CW00859392

Solo Act

Helen Dunwoodie

CORGI BOOKS

SOLO ACT
A CORGI BOOK : 0 552 545244

First publication in Great Britain

PRINTING HISTORY
Corgi edition published 1997

Set in 11/12pt Monotype Plantin by Kestrel Data, Exeter, Devon.

Corgi Books are published by Transworld Publishers Ltd, 61–63 Uxbridge Road, London W5 5SA, in Australia by Transworld Publishers (Australia) Pty Ltd, 15–25 Helles Avenue, Moorebank, NSW 2170, and in New Zealand by Transworld Publishers (NZ) Ltd, 3 William Pickering Drive, Albany, Auckland.

Made and printed in Great Britain by Cox and Wyman Ltd, Reading, Berks.

For Anna and Katy, daughters and divas,
and for the nine muses,
Shona, Madeleine, Ellie,
Kelly, Monica, Polly,
Holly, Emma and Vicki

Chapter One

It was the moment I loved. I moved centre stage, looked up appealingly into the spotlight, clasped my hands, and began to sing:

> 'I can't tell my mother
> That I'm so afraid—'

I was lost in the part of Effie, terrified of what lay ahead, and begging the audience for their pity. I lowered my hands to my crinoline and took a few more steps forward so that the spot was obliged to follow me, leaving the rest of the cast in the shadows.

> 'I can't tell my husband
> Of the price to be paid—'

An undercurrent of sobs ran through my voice. By now some of the spectators would be reaching for their hankies.

'For heaven's sake, girl, stop that wretched *acting*! Just sing. You know what singing is, don't you? It's the thing you *can* do. Just stand there. Open your mouth. Sing. Then stop. End of story.'

I broke off in mid-note. Our director was standing in the empty hall, waving his script at me. I couldn't see him properly for the lights, so I aimed my words at the flapping white paper.

'But *Jimmy*, what about the *sub-text*? In this scene

I have to establish Effie's character *and* convey her horror of—'

'Iris, sweetheart, I'm not disagreeing with you, but for the moment could you please forget the heavy drama and just sing?'

I clenched my lace-mittened hands. I had been the star of the Christmas show since I was fourteen, first as Anne in *Anne of Green Gables* and then, last year, as Maria, in *The Sound of Music*. I wasn't going to let some stuck-up failed actor boss me around.

'And go back to where you were. None of this sidling forward and taking the spot with you.'

Despite myself, I moved back a couple of steps.

'Further, further!'

I crept back until I was almost on top of Dinah and Morven, who were perched on their Victorian sofa, holding their breaths lest Jimmy turn on them for fidgeting or slipping out of character.

'That's it. Don't move. Now sing. With your looks that's all you need to do. From the beginning, Fay.'

Mrs Reece, the head music teacher, brought in the school orchestra, and I sang my big solo deadpan, with neither gestures nor expression.

If that's what he wants, I'll let him have it, I thought.

I was burning up with anger inside. This had been my main emotion during every moment of the production, from the first drama group meeting right up until today, the dress rehearsal. It was bad enough that dear Miss Kerr, our old drama and singing teacher, had retired, to be replaced by this egomaniac; even worse, he was one of these directors who believe in 'letting the script *evolve*, with all the cast *contributing input*'.

I mean, with Miss Kerr, we knew where we were.

She'd announce the show, hold auditions, put up a cast list, and then we'd rehearse through October and November and, finally, dazzle our parents during the last week of term. And as she was a real fan of old musicals, she always chose one of the classics, something which everyone would enjoy.

Jimmy, however, wanted to do something meaningful. Meaningful but fun.

'These qualities can go together,' he had said at our first meeting, lounging back against the platform and tossing his long black pony-tail.

Several girls sighed, while the boys either sniggered or looked envious.

Quite a lot is allowed at our school, but not pony-tails on boys. Randal says this is sexist, and campaigned to get the rules changed, but Mrs Jennings, our headmistress, said that although Randal was in the right, the parents wouldn't stand for it. So Jimmy's hairstyle made him extra alluring and exotic in most people's eyes. But not in mine.

'We can put on a show which says something about our society *and* which people will enjoy watching.'

'You mean, like they won't notice it's got a message?' This was Dinah, who throws herself into everything, whether she understands it or not.

'Subliminal?' said Rachel, who is our resident intellectual.

'No,' said Jimmy. 'There's nothing wrong with letting an audience know they're thinking. Look at *Les Mis* or *Miss Saigon* – musicals have changed a lot since *The Sound of Music.*'

I felt myself going hot all over. I don't know if he had picked out that show on purpose, but I wasn't going to let him make fun of it. I'd loved every moment of being Maria, and I'd cried when I took off my dirndl for the last time.

'You can hardly say that *The Sound of Music* doesn't have a message,' I said, looking straight at him. 'It's about the triumph of music over oppression.'

'Well, granted, dear – what's your name?'

'Iris,' I said in my best, rounded tones.

'Well, Iris,' said Jimmy, in an odious, actressy voice, almost as though he were making fun of me, 'well, Iris, you have made an intelligent point. Would anyone agree with Iris?'

He scanned the group. People looked at one another, no-one keen to sound silly by giving the wrong opinion.

Then Randal, who was stretched out on the floor, raised himself sufficiently to say: 'Because something's silly isn't to say it's not true.'

'Aha, explain!' Jimmy turned to face Randal, his pony-tail, held back in a cherry-red buncher, whisking after him. The buncher matched his T-shirt, which he wore with loose black trousers and what seemed to be black dancing pumps.

Randal looked bored, as he always does when he is about to be intelligent, and said: 'I mean, look at the panda. It exists, but what could be sillier?' And he raised a beautiful brown eyebrow in my direction.

Everyone laughed. Alabama Bywaters, who is my best friend, hit Randal over the head with a folder. 'Randal, you're such a show-off.'

'No, that was very well put.' Jimmy beamed at Randal. He was obviously going to be one of those male teachers who have already decided that boys are smarter and more worth listening to than girls.

'*Sound of Music*, like the panda, exists. And like the panda, it's remarkably silly.'

He pranced round in a circle, held his baggy trousers out at the knee, and with a coy, innocent expression on his face, burst into 'The hills are alive with the sound of music'.

It was incredible. He became, he actually became Maria – but a Maria who was wickedly just over the top, just too good to be true.

The girls screamed with laughter and the boys hooted and cat-called. I was blushing with rage and mortification. One or two of my special friends – Aly, Rachel – looked at me sympathetically. But they still laughed.

'I don't think it's fair to make fun of the shows we did with Miss Kerr. They were very successful.' I managed to keep my voice from trembling when I spoke.

Jimmy looked at me with his large, dark eyes. 'You don't mean to tell me that *you* did *Sound of Music*?'

Several people nodded. The laughter had died down.

'And I bet you played Maria?'

'Yes,' I said.

'Oops!' Jimmy slapped himself on the wrist, and the laughter broke out all over again.

I didn't know which possibility was worse: that he hadn't cared enough to find out which shows we'd done; or that he'd known all along and was teasing me. I made up my mind, there and then, that I wasn't going to co-operate with this man. And I'd start by keeping my mouth shut for the rest of the afternoon.

Jimmy was now in full flood about his wonderful drama method. 'Brain-storming session . . .

everyone have a say . . . something which affects your own lives.'

I watched him, letting his words drift past me. He was certainly incredibly attractive. All that black hair, olive skin and a nose that, in profile, made an absolutely straight line with his brow. As he spoke he seemed to give off energy, rising on the balls of his feet and moving his hands all the time, as if he were drawing pictures for us in the air.

Mrs Jennings had said we were lucky to get Jimmy Garcia to replace Miss Kerr. Apparently he also taught in some kids' theatre workshop south of the river, and at a drama college. Thinks he's a big pro, bringing real theatre to a bunch of amateurs, I thought angrily. *And* I bet his name's not really Garcia. He probably picked it to suit his image.

'Come on, give me some ideas.' Jimmy was now crouching on the ground with a huge pad of paper and a giant marker which he'd taken from his bag. 'It doesn't matter how silly – give yourselves permission to go completely over the top. That way we get maybe a hundred rotten ideas, six fairly good, and one so absolutely brilliant it makes theatrical history.'

'Drug abuse.'

'The homeless.'

'A single mother struggling to bring up her kids.'

People were getting into this really quickly. As they yelled out suggestions, Jimmy scrawled them down.

'Famine.'

'The imigration laws and deportees.'

Our school is very hot on politics.

'OK, OK.' Jimmy was writing as fast as he could.

'Plenty of ideas there. But they all have something in common. Who can tell me what it is?'

He looked around. Silence. The feeling in the room reminded me of kindergarten, when we'd all wanted to win a gold star by giving the right answer. Already, in one session, Jimmy had made everyone – everyone except me – desperate to win his approval.

'They're all contemporary issues.' Even Randal, lying on his back with his long arms folded under his head, was giving in to Jimmy's charm.

'Uhuh. One. Something else?'

'Mmm – it's like—' Janine Boswell had never spoken up in drama before, so we all turned round in surprise. Her plain little face turned a painful red. 'It's – none of these things affects any of us personally. I mean, no-one here's homeless, or a single parent.'

There was some giggling, and William said loudly: 'Yet,' but Jimmy cut across this with an absolute whoop of approval.

'Exactly! None of you privileged kids knows what it's like to live in a cardboard box. So let's have some ideas based on your own experience.'

People were more reluctant to speak up now that Jimmy had moved the discussion closer to home.

Then Dinah bounced in, leading the way as usual. 'Peer pressure, people doing things because they want to fit in with their friends.'

'A-levels,' said Morven, glancing at Rachel, her academic rival. Morven hates her because Rachel always comes out top, quite effortlessly.

'Yes, working so hard one cracks under the strain,' drawled Randal, so lazily that everyone laughed again.

'Divorce.'

'Family quarrels.'

'But if we do a show about family problems, everyone in the audience will think it's about them.' This was Janine again. Jimmy's approval seemed to have caused a total character change.

'Wait.' Rachel, who never speaks until she has something important to say, raised her head. Her curly hair, which she wears pushed up into a bunch with two combs, floated above her serious face like a small black cloud. 'I know something that definitely will affect half of the people here, and half of the audience.'

Some of the girls and all the boys groaned. Rachel is well known for her involvement in women's rights, so whenever she began: 'At least half the people here', we knew what to expect.

'Don't tell me – a biopic: *Emmeline Pankhurst and Her Struggle for the Vote*,' said Adrian in disgust.

'If we do the death of that woman who was run down by the horse, bags I be the horse,' said William, bursting into a horse impression.

'No, I wasn't thinking of that,' said Rachel, still perfectly serious. She never rises to teasing or gets provoked into side issues. 'What I was thinking about was childbirth.'

A lot of us, including some girls, made surprised or disapproving noises, but Jimmy nodded eagerly. 'Yeah, yeah, that's a really intriguing idea.'

'I did a social studies project last term on the proposal to close the maternity wing in the local hospital. This would cause a lot of problems for women around here – but then I began to think: these problems are nothing compared to what all pregnant women suffered up until a short time ago. So I did a bit of extra reading.'

This is also typical of Rachel. She ferrets into a

subject until she knows it inside out. Now she was speaking with such knowledge and fervour that she actually began to carry her reluctant audience along with her.

'It's not just that the mortality rate in childbirth was so high, but until the development of anaesthesia and, later, natural childbirth techniques, women had to bear terrible pain. But what I found fascinating was the opposition to the use of anaesthesia in childbirth. Mostly from men, but from some women too.'

'But how could people possibly object?' said Alabama.

Rachel held a dramatic pause. Then, her black eyes glistening, she snapped out: 'The Bible. It says that God cursed Eve with the pain of childbirth as a punishment for eating the forbidden apple.'

'People really believed that?' said Dinah, shaking her head in amazement so that her crescent moon ear-rings got tangled in her hair. 'How totally primitive.'

'Yes, a lot of Victorians thought that the Bible was literally true, and therefore they believed that any attempt to relieve women's suffering was contrary to God's will.'

There was a tremendous outcry from the girls. Rachel really had their attention now. I even found myself becoming interested, although I was still determined not to be won over.

'I think we could do a really topical show on changing attitudes,' she continued.

'But this sounds like a real women's issue,' protested Adrian, not surprisingly, as he is our best actor. He had made a wonderful Captain von Trapp, powerful and authoritative.

'Yeah, perhaps you girls ought to form one of

those women's theatre groups called something like Hag's Revenge or Furies Unleashed, and we boys'll do our own show. I'll play a house-husband who's tempted by a series of visiting work-women.'

Rachel ignored William, who is always trying to get a rise out of her, and addressed Adrian. 'No, men were very much involved. It was a Scottish doctor, Dr Simpson, who pioneered the use of anaesthesia in childbirth.'

Adrian began to look interested, seeing a good part for himself.

'And we could still have music,' said Aly. She was ruffling up her fair, frizzy hair as she always does when she's excited, until it stood out straight like thistledown. 'Perhaps a chorus of Victorian women in crinolines singing "O Welcome, Anaesthesia!" and then a chorus of men disagreeing with them.'

'Yes, we've got something here! C'mon, more ideas!' Jimmy was kneeling over his notepad in a graceful loop, his marker flying over the paper in huge twirls and swirls. 'More, more! As wild as you like!' He looked up and grinned. '*Anaesthesia! A New Musical*!' I like it, kids, I like it!'

Chapter Two

Naturally, I'd begun by declaring that I wouldn't audition. Nothing, I said to Aly, would induce me to work with Jimmy. And while Rachel's idea might be interesting intellectually, it was scarcely *theatre*.

'But, Iris, we can't do a show without you!' Aly put down her coffee and leant earnestly across the kitchen table. It was a couple of days later and we were having an after-school snack of *cappuccino*, low-fat cheese and Ryvita. The *cappuccino* had been made with my mother's latest kitchen acquisition. She really dislikes cooking but has this belief that, if she buys enough gadgets, she will be transformed into a cordon bleu chef.

I skimmed the froth from my cup and sipped it from the spoon. 'You can easily do without me. Dinah and Sarah can sing, and Morven wouldn't be bad if only she'd learn to breathe properly.'

'Oh, don't be stupid, you know you'll give in in the end. You couldn't bear not to be in a show.'

That's the trouble with having a best friend. They know you better than you know yourself. Aly and I have been friends since kindergarten, when she was a tiny scrap with wild blond hair which wouldn't stay in its bunchers, and I had bright ginger curls. Besides our weird hair, we also had in common the silliest names in the class. I was romantically called Iris, after the messenger of the Greek gods, and Aly was named in honour of the black children who were jailed in Alabama for trying to go to white schools. Her mother saw a documentary about this while she was pregnant, and it made a great impression on her. If I'd been called after a protest movement, I'm sure I would've become some sort of vandal in revenge, but Aly actually seems to have been favourably influenced by her name. For instance, when we were in Primary 2 she confessed at once when she let the class hamster escape. And she only let him out because she thought it unfair to keep him in a cage. She is much more like Rachel than she is like me, but for some reason she and I go on being best friends. She tries to turn me into a nobler character and I try to make her lighten up.

'And we need you,' she now continued. 'You're by far the best singer.'

This wasn't just flattery, for while I love acting, singing is my real talent. And my voice has been well trained – until she retired, Miss Kerr had been giving me private lessons. If only she hadn't moved to Bournemouth! Now I'd have to find a new singing teacher as well as dealing with Jimmy and his crazy ideas.

'So what?' I said. 'It doesn't sound as though there's going to be as much music in this show.'

'Yes, there is! If you'd only condescended to come along yesterday you'd know what was happening. Dinah and Adrian and Randal are going to write the lyrics and a friend of Jimmy's is going to compose original music for us. Blake Evans. Jimmy says he's going to be a really big name some day.'

'If Jimmy says so, he must be all right then.'

'Iris, you're not going to be nasty about Jimmy for ever, are you? It's so petty.'

Aly has a little pointed face like an elf, with very fair skin which, when she gets angry, goes bright pink. This was happening now.

'Well,' I said, 'well, I don't like him because he just shows off the entire time.'

'You mean you don't like him because he made fun of *The Sound of Music*. But he didn't know we'd done it.'

'Huh.'

'Anyway, you can't let the group down. Your feelings shouldn't matter beside the good of the show.'

This is the sort of thing I meant when I said that Aly was influenced by her name – although I suppose the fact that her parents are very earnest, political types has something to do with it.

'At least come to the next rehearsal,' she said. 'It's really good. Rachel's given us photocopies of her notes and we do improvisations based on them. William was a scream as Queen Victoria.'

'What on earth has Queen Victoria got to do with anaesthesia?'

'She was a pioneer, believe it or not. She insisted on being given chloroform when her last two children were born, and that made it respectable. William was so good that Jimmy's going to keep his piece in the show.'

'If he's going to do this thing of having boys playing women's parts then there's no point in my auditioning, is there?'

'But that's just because William was so hilarious. Come on, Iris, Jimmy's never heard you sing. When he does, you can bet he'll have Blake Evans write a special song for you.'

The thought of Jimmy being incredibly impressed by my voice was tempting. I imagined him looking up from his notes, the pen falling from his hand as he listened, entranced. 'I didn't know you could sing like that,' he'd say. 'Iris, I'm going to make you a star! And I'm sorry I made fun of Maria.'

While I dreamt, Aly was still talking. She could see I was weakening. 'Look, we're doing more improvisations tomorrow. They count as acting auditions, and the singing auditions are next week.'

'I suppose I might come.'

'Yes, you will. You know you won't be able to keep away.'

I had to grin at her. She knew that not even my dislike of Jimmy would keep me away in the end. I loved everything to do with being in a show, the excitement, the shared jokes and dramas, the eventual applause. I even loved long boring rehearsals and learning my lines and being too tired to get up in the morning.

When Aly had left I sat on in the kitchen and brooded. Our kitchen used to be hi-tech, all cold gleaming white cabinets and stainless steel, but Maggie, my mother, had these all ripped out a couple of years ago and replaced with the country kitchen look. Now we have pine dressers with blue-and-white plates on the shelves, and rows of copper saucepans which we hardly ever use. I suppose it's so long since Maggie left the farm where she grew up that she feels it's now safe to revert to a homely atmosphere. I like it. It's much easier to brood in a rocking chair than balanced on a bit of Italian plastic.

It was very quiet. Our flat is the top floor of a villa in one of the leafy streets behind Chalk Farm, so except for the occasional car passing, there's no noise.

Jimmy had been right about one thing. We kids didn't have much experience of life. We all lived in comfortable houses, like mine, and we went to our private school, and by and by most of us would go on to university. Of course, there were difficulties – for example, Janine's mother was very ill, and several of us had divorced parents – but somehow, these family tragedies were smothered by our lined curtains and thick carpets and central heating.

I thought about my own life. Maggie and I had our beautiful flat, yet we quarrelled all the time, mainly about exams and singing and my eventual career. Perhaps it would've been easier if there hadn't been just the two of us. When I was very little, before I met Aly, I used to pester Maggie for a sister; I couldn't understand it when she said she couldn't have more babies without a daddy. She had me, didn't she? But after Aly and I became friends I didn't really need a sister any more, although I still had the pressure of being successful Maggie's only daughter.

I sat and rocked for a bit until Maggie came in, interrupting a fantasy in which Jimmy's friend wrote me an amazing aria because he was so impressed by my voice. I heard her come down the hall, her high heels tapping on the polished wood, the tap changing to a patter as she crossed one of the Persian rugs which she collected.

'Iris, have you begun your homework yet?'

She had started nagging almost before she'd opened the kitchen door. I whisked my French reader out of my bag and waved it.

'Behold, the hardworking daughter.'

She clipped towards me, preceded by wafts of Estée Lauder's Cinnabar. 'That looks like a novel.'

'It is a novel, but it's in French. We have to discuss it in class tomorrow.'

Maggie caught my triumphant expression. 'What else do you have to do?' she snapped.

I sighed. We go through this almost every night. 'This French. Maths. And I'll need to begin my report on Jane Austen. Do I think *Persuasion* has any relevance to today's society?'

'That'll keep you busy. What time do you want to eat?'

'I don't mind. Whatever suits you. Are you going out?'

'Me – go out? Impossible, I've got all this to deal with.'

She gestured towards her briefcase, which she had laid down on the table amongst my school stuff. It's made from glossy black leather and gleams like some sort of weapon.

'Shall I make supper, then?' I said.

'No, I'll do it. You get on with your work.'

Maggie fetched herself some spring water from the fridge and then leant against the counter, sipping it. As usual, she looked very smart, expensive, and in control, with her beautiful haircut and her little black suit. Maggie buys new designer suits every year, always black. However, despite all the effort she puts into her appearance, she can't escape from looking exactly like Gran, who is a dumpy little countrywoman with wide hips and big hands and feet. I look totally different from both of them, with my long, dark-red hair and slanting navy-blue eyes. And I don't know whom I resemble.

'It only means putting something in the oven,' I said.

Maggie and I don't cook much. We usually just

heat up something from the freezer and make a salad.

'No, your work's more important. Still, I suppose you'll have more time for studying if you're not doing the show this year.'

I tilted the rocking chair backwards and forwards. 'Oh, I don't know. I might do it after all.'

'Iris, we've discussed this. You know I think that acting takes up too much of your time. I was delighted that you'd decided to be sensible and give it a miss this time.

'It didn't affect my work before.'

'But the other years weren't so important. If you want to get into a good university you have to work seriously from now on.'

'I am working seriously!' I thumped the French book down on top of my maths. 'Anyway, this show's going to be different. I won't be playing a big lead role. This is going to be an "equal opportunity production",' I said, quoting Jimmy.

'But wouldn't you mind that, darling?' said Maggie. 'You must admit, you're used to being the star.'

Of course I minded.

'No,' I said. 'It's for the good of the show.'

Chapter Three

I was still feeling sulky about Jimmy and his famous improvisations, so when I turned up at the next rehearsal I decided to keep in the background. This wasn't difficult because, rather to my surprise, no-one apart from Aly and Rachel seemed to notice that I hadn't been to the last one. They were all too busy fussing round Jimmy, who was organizing us into groups. I was put with Adrian, Janine, Sarah and Andy, and Jimmy told us to act a scene in which a husband is told by the doctor that either his wife or his child can be saved, and then asked, which does he choose?

'That seems a bit far-fetched,' said Adrian, pushing back his curly brown hair.

'No, not in those days,' said Rachel. 'Childbirth was much more dangerous then than it is now, so a man could be asked to make that decision.'

'It would keep women up to the mark if they knew that their husbands could casually dispose of them like that,' observed Randal. 'No bad thing.'

All the girls groaned. I ignored him and went with my group to the centre of the platform.

'Two minutes to discuss who's who, then jump in with both feet,' said Jimmy.

Today he was wearing a turquoise shirt, and his pony-tail was held back with a little strip of plaited leather.

We decided – or rather, I decided and no-one disagreed with me – that I would be the dying woman, Adrian my distraught husband, Andy the doctor, Sarah the nurse, and Janine, because she's so small, would be my little daughter, brought in to bid me farewell.

I lay down on a row of chairs, feeling cross and unco-operative. I decided to get the whole thing over with by dying as quickly and quietly as possible.

However, I'd reckoned without Adrian. He takes rehearsals very seriously and always stays completely inside the character he's playing. So when he took my limp hand and looked down at me, his gaze was filled with such pain and consternation that I couldn't help responding.

'Save our child!' I gasped. 'We have had so many happy years, my beloved – let the child live—' and I broke off with a cry of pain.

'Let me have a few words with you, sir,' said Andy, drawing Adrian away from my bedside.

They stood downstage, discussing my case, leaving me to moan in the background. I let my moans rise to a scream. Then I sobbed out: 'My little Emily, I must see her one last time. Fetch her, nurse, please.'

Adrian rushed back to my side. 'No, my love, do not distress yourself. You will see Emily tomorrow.'

I was beginning to enjoy this. 'Tomorrow will be too late!' I cried.

'No, no!' Jimmy let out his own howl of pain. We all stopped and stared at him. He was trampling round in circles with his arms clasped over his head like someone being attacked by a swarm of bees.

'God give me patience! If this is going on till Christmas there *will* be a dead body stretched out on that stage, and Iris, love, it'll be yours! You're not feeling, you're *acting*.'

I sat up on my death bed and looked at him coldly. 'I thought that was what I was *meant* to be doing.'

'Let me ask you a question. You're adoring being on your death bed, aren't you?'

I didn't answer, but I felt myself turning a bright, embarrassing red. I have the sort of freckled skin that shows the faintest trace of a blush.

'Now think: you're never going to see your husband or your little girl again. Who's going to look after her? Will she lie awake, night after night, crying for you? Will she keep asking when you're coming home?'

My eyes filled with tears. I think Jimmy knew that I was crying for my own hurt feelings rather than for pitiful little Emily, but he said: 'That's more like it. Use that feeling, not your pleasure in being centre stage. Now carry on. Adrian, see if you can hold what you're doing. It's good.'

I lay back on my chairs and let the others act around me. When Janine was led in by the nurse, she dragged behind and refused to approach me. If I'd been playing that part, I would've run up to the bed and made a big scene out of saying goodbye, but I suddenly understood that she was behaving just as a frightened little girl would do. She wanted to hide rather than see her mother transformed by pain.

When we had finished and Jimmy was giving us our notes, I found that I'd been right. 'Very nice indeed,' he said to Janine. 'A very good piece of observation.'

She blushed even more than I had done and turned away. Then I remembered: Janine's own mother had just come out of hospital. I caught Randal and Aly both looking at me, and I realized how tactless I'd been in making her play the part of the daughter.

Jimmy seemed to guess that something was wrong, and he swept on quickly to the next scene.

'I feel so bad about letting Janine be the little girl,' I said to Aly later, as we came out of the school gates together.

The hall is in what's still known as the boys' building, although the boys' and girls' departments, which were separate in the distant days when our school was founded by a Victorian scholar named Dr Blacklock and his progressive sisters, have been joined together for years now. However, it means that we have three separate buildings, two old, and the new science block, so a lot of time can be wasted by dawdling from one class to another.

Aly and I turned right, away from the main road, and began to walk down the quiet street. I kicked a pebble along the pavement, and Aly kicked it back, like we used to do when we were little and wore Clarks sandals.

'I just didn't think,' I said.

Aly said nothing, and I let the pebble roll into the gutter.

'Well,' I continued, defending myself against her silent accusation, 'it would be easier to remember that something's wrong if Janine ever talked about it. I mean, we wouldn't even know that her mother was ill if she hadn't had to explain why she was taking so much time off school.'

'Yes, well, but we do know,' said Aly. 'I'm not blaming you, Iris, but you might've remembered.'

'If that's not blaming, I don't know what is.'

'No, it was a mistake. I'm not blaming you for a mistake. It's not as though you set out deliberately to hurt her feelings.'

'Thank you very much,' I said, increasing the pace.

'Oh, come on, Iris, don't be angry.'

It was my turn to keep quiet. Aly doesn't like quarrels, so I knew that she'd make up with me before we reached my gate.

However, after a moment or two, what she said was: 'I just mean – how could you *forget* that Janine's mother's got cancer?'

The horrible word lay between us, solid and heavy, like AIDS or pollution or nuclear disaster. I shrugged my shoulders under my blue school blazer. 'Well, I don't think it's fair of you to expect me to treat her differently – in fact, if I were her, I'd hate to think that everyone was only being nice because they were sorry for me.'

I didn't want to be talking about Janine at all. I'd wanted to complain to Aly – who, after all, was *my* best friend – about Jimmy. Miss Kerr had never found fault with my acting, so why was he being so hard on me? My anger at Jimmy and my guilt over the way I'd treated Janine made me speak harshly. 'Honestly, Aly, you're always so worried about people, and half the time I expect they don't want you to bother.'

Of course, I really wanted her to be concerned about *me*, but it seemed a bit trivial to moan about what had happened to me during drama when what was happening to Janine and her mother was so much worse.

Aly didn't reply and I knew I'd hurt her feelings. Janine, and now Aly too. I stamped along, cross and sorry for myself.

Despite the speed at which we were now walking, someone was catching us up.

'You might've waited for me.'

It was Randal. His legs are so long that he takes one stride to two of mine and about four of Aly's. And that's without having to hurry, something he never does. He came up to us, fair hair flopping over his face, old canvas rucksack swinging. All Randal's possessions are as ancient as possible: it's part of his languid, aristocrat pose, as though he simply can't be bothered to go out and buy new stuff.

'Why didn't you wait?' he said. 'What've I done to make myself so unpopular?'

'You don't need to *do* anything,' I snapped. 'Existing is quite sufficient.'

In the far-off days when I was fifteen and he was sixteen – in fact, a whole year ago – I'd been madly in love with Randal, a memory which now makes me writhe with embarrassment. However, just like one of those sad old movies full of misunderstandings and partings, he didn't even notice me until I'd met someone else – Rachel's French cousin, Jean-Paul, who was staying with her family for the summer. I was soon so entranced by Jean-Paul, who smelt of Gauloises and called me his *p'tite amie*, that I'd no time for stiff, blond, English Randal. Of course, the European Alliance, as Rachel called it, didn't survive Jean-Paul's return to France, but we still write friendly letters and he sent me a wonderful silk scarf last Christmas, dark purple and mauve. 'The colours of your name' he'd written on the card.

I couldn't imagine Randal ever being so romantic.

We now had an uneasy relationship in which we

were always either arguing, or else making sarcastic comments about the other's taste, appearance, and character. Yet, as Alabama and Rachel kept pointing out, neither of us had got involved with anyone else.

'Oh, you're not intelligent enough to be taken seriously,' he now said, loping along beside me. 'Fortunately, I'm immensely popular with most other people, which is more than can be said for you. Didn't Jimmy just tear into your acting?'

I turned my face away. 'I can take professional criticism,' I said airily. 'It's when the director doesn't bother to criticize your work that you've got to worry.'

It was true that Jimmy hadn't found much to say about Randal's acting. Randal is always a bit awkward on stage. He looks good, but he's too self-conscious to lose himself in a part the way Adrian does.

'I'd rather be ignored than told I'm an incitement to murder.'

'It was simply a figure of speech,' I said.

'I'm surprised you're taking this so calmly. I was expecting you to be sobbing on Aly's shoulder and saying you'd rather die than be in the show.'

This was so nearly true that, if a car had come along at that moment, I would've been tempted to push him under it.

However, the road remained empty so I said, as steadily as I could: 'Rubbish. I wouldn't be such a baby.'

'So you're going to the music auditions, then?'

'Naturally.'

'Of course Iris is going,' said Aly loyally, as though we hadn't just been fighting. 'You know we can't do without her.'

'Oh, we all know what a star Iris is,' said Randal, talking over my head to Aly. 'Pity it doesn't make her nicer. I mean, look at that trick she pulled on Janine.'

'I did not pull a trick on Janine!' I shouted, swinging round and facing them both. 'For heaven's sake, Randal, I just made a mistake. OK, I forgot about her mother. That's hardly a crime. I just *forgot*!'

'Iris didn't mean to be tactless.' Aly came to my defence at once.

'And anyway,' I continued, 'since when have *you* been so concerned about Janine? I've never even seen you speak to her.'

'I might begin right now,' he replied. 'We could form a support group: the Victims of Mad Iris Trust, VOMIT for short!' And he turned off down his own street, laughing at his sophisticated wit.

I walked on at a furious pace, with Aly pattering behind me.

'I'm going to kill him some day,' I said. 'I'm really going to kill him.'

'The angrier you get, the more he'll tease you. He only does it because you get mad. He never bothers Rachel because she just ignores him.'

'But Rachel's not a Leo. You should never tease Leos.' And I tossed my long red mane.

Aly's serious parents have brought her up to disbelieve in astrology, so she just said: 'You mean, no-one should tease *you*.'

Then, being a total Pisces, always eager to calm troubled waters, she continued: 'Don't be angry, Iris, it's not worth it. And you'll really come to the singing auditions?'

'Of course I'm going to the wretched auditions!' I yelled. 'I've just said so, haven't I?'

'I'm sorry.'

I didn't reply until we'd reached my gate, and then, because I can't bear to quarrel with Aly any more than she can bear to quarrel with me, I hugged her and said: 'I'm sorry too. I suppose.'

' 'Course you are. Goodnight.'

And Aly carried on down the street, her bouncy blond hair catching the light. I watched her go and then walked up the gravel path which, lined with thick, boring bushes, leads around the side of the house to our entrance, an outside staircase with a glass roof over it. As I climbed the steps and let myself in I thought, what did it matter if other people didn't like me or admire me? I had Aly for my best friend. And that meant I could afford to be generous. I'd really try to be nicer to Janine from now on.

Chapter Four

The singing auditions were a walk-over. Jimmy didn't actually fall off his chair with amazement when he heard my voice, but he did look up from his notes and stare at me for a moment with a completely new look on his face. A look of surprise – and, yes, respect.

I pretended not to notice as I soared up easily to a high note. Remembering Jimmy's approving remarks on *Les Miserables,* I'd decided to sing 'Just a Little Rain', but I'd asked Mrs Reece, who was accompanying, to move it up a few semi-tones so that I could display my top notes. When I'd finished I nodded coolly to Jimmy and to his composer friend, Blake Evans, who was a surprisingly conventional-looking, chubby, check-suited young man, and strolled out of the room. I knew I'd made an impression.

'That'll show him,' I said to myself as I walked home. 'Just let him dare not cast me.'

However, when we went along to the next rehearsal Jimmy didn't have an actual cast list for us.

'OK, kids,' he said, sitting down cross-legged in the middle of the group and opening the huge, battered leather bag he always carried. 'OK, as this show is evolving as we go along I don't have a definite cast list for you' – there were moans and grumbles, which he ignored '—just some ideas. We may introduce new characters, or I may decide to swap people around. So don't be disappointed if your name isn't on this list – you may still get a part. And remember, in a show like this, everybody is important.' And he might have been glancing in my direction when he concluded: 'There are no stars.'

This is what drama teachers always say, and everybody knows that it's rubbish. There is no way in which a member of the chorus is going to be as important as someone with a leading role. As Jimmy seemed to look at me I thought, for the first time: What if he drops me? What if I find myself in the chorus? Could I bear to have people pitying me, or laughing behind my back – me – Iris Campion, the leading lady of Blacklock's Theatre Group?

I concentrated on looking cool and unconcerned as Jimmy drew out a sheet of paper, held it up, and then, very, very slowly, unfolded it. What a showman, I thought; he had everyone staring at that paper as though it held the secret of the universe, rather than a few names.

He kept the tension for just the right number of beats, and then began to read. As we'd expected, Adrian was to play Dr Simpson, Dinah was to be his wife, Aly and Morven two of her friends, and Janine his daughter. When Janine heard her name, her head jerked up and she stared at Jimmy, her brown eyes wide open. She had never had a speaking part before.

Jimmy paused and looked at her. 'Yes, you,' he said. And he winked. 'You can do it.'

I was outraged. Why was he making such a fuss over mousy Janine, with her straggly fawn hair and long nose? Perhaps he'd found out about her mother and now he, too, felt sorry for her?

Jimmy had begin reading again, so I quickly turned my attention back to him. William was Queen Victoria, Randal a disapproving clergyman, Rachel one of the first women doctors – I waited for my name. As he went down the list I just could not believe that he was going to miss me out. I began to plan what I would do if he had. I would get up and march out of the hall. No, that would draw attention to myself. I'd wait until the end of the rehearsal and then confront him and ask if he felt threatened by my talent – after all, I *was* the best singer—

'Now, Iris, what are we to do with you?'

I jumped, just as Janine had done. Jimmy looked amused. Like Randal, he seemed to enjoy teasing me. He fluttered the list like a fan, drawing out the suspense. '*Blake* liked your voice,' he said, emphasizing the composer's name. 'He wants to write something which would suit it.'

I suppressed a grin of pure, triumphant delight. My fantasy of having a song specially written for me was actually coming true!

'Oh, I can't take much credit for my voice,' I said modestly. 'I've got a wonderful new singing teacher, Matthew Stoller. Most of his pupils are professional singers.'

I had written to Miss Kerr for advice and she'd suggested Mr Stoller. I'd only been going to him for a few weeks, but already my technique was improving.

Jimmy ignored my self-deprecating remarks. 'The only problem is,' he continued, 'where are we going to fit her in? Ideas anyone? Where are we going to put Iris, the jewel in our musical crown?'

Before I could decide whether Jimmy were being complimentary or sarcastic, Janine burst in. 'Jimmy,' she said, 'I've got an idea. Why shouldn't one of Mrs Simpson's friends be a young married woman who's pregnant for the first time but terrified of actually having a baby? Then, if Iris played that part, she could sing a really tragic song, revealing her feelings.'

I loved it! I hate to admit it, but little Janine had come up with a brilliant, dramatic idea. I could just see myself, beautiful and afraid, moving the audience to tears. Everyone else was pretty impressed too.

'Of course!' cried Rachel. 'Then, when she has the baby painlessly, due to the miracle of anaesthesia, she can have a song of thanksgiving.'

'Janine, that's fantastic.' Aly reached over to touch her shoulder. Janine smiled back at her. 'You're a genius,' said Aly.

I thought perhaps that was going a bit far. I turned away from them to Jimmy. 'Sure,' I said, as calmly as I could. 'It sounds a good idea.'

Jimmy didn't seem to be as enthusiastic as the rest of the group. 'Yes,' he said slowly, 'it's an excellent idea, Janine, I'm not knocking it, but what I wonder, Iris, what I wonder is how you'd deal with a dramatic part like that.'

I stared at him in surprise. Of course I could deal with it! 'Well, dramatically,' I said lightly, turning it into a joke.

He didn't laugh. 'Just what I was afraid of.'

I knew I must be looking like a dying goldfish with my mouth open, so I snapped it shut and returned his gaze with silent dignity. Then he *did* laugh.

'Oh, I love the aggrieved glare!' he said. 'What

have I done to offend the Duchess? Never mind, Iris, sweetie, we'll try it out. Just concentrate on the singing and let the acting take care of itself.'

Why on earth was he banging on about my acting? I'll show him, I vowed to myself. I'll show him what real acting looks like.

I smiled sweetly. 'Thank you, Jimmy,' I said. 'I'm looking forward to working with you.'

He gave me a very swift, odd look, almost as though he were about to start laughing again, but before I could meet it, he'd turned back to the group.

'Now, darlings,' he said. A very pleased, smug expression had come over his face. 'Now, darlings, Uncle Jimmy has a little treat for you.'

I found myself gazing back eagerly like all the others.

'Yes,' he continued, 'I know already that you're all going to work your little butts off because, if you don't, you're out. But just to encourage you, here's a tiny idea I had. I think – I think that if we make a success of this show we could take it up to the Edinburgh Festival next summer and present it on the Fringe!'

Jimmy looked round eagerly for our reactions, but was met by blank faces. 'Well, come *on*, isn't that an exciting idea? Don't you want to take part in one of the world's biggest cultural events?'

He was starting to look disappointed and irritated, like a little boy when the grown-ups fail to laugh at his jokes. Several people spoke up hurriedly.

'But isn't the Edinburgh Festival just for opera and ballet?' said William.

'Or professional theatre groups?' added Adrian.

'And what is the Fringe, anyway?' said Dinah,

putting the question that the rest of us were too scared to ask for fear of looking totally ignorant.

Morven said, with an irritating air of worldly knowledge: 'Well, I went to Edinburgh a couple of years ago with my parents' – her parents are big classical music fans – 'and my mother said the Fringe wasn't worth bothering about. It's just little shows on the edge of the real festival, put on by students or amateur dramatic societies.'

Jimmy put his arms around his head in his favourite posture of despair and moaned. Then he sat up and said: 'You pampered, spoilt, middle-class *brats* – how dare you be so pig- ignorant? Your parents buy you books and computers and TV sets, don't they? You have access to all this *knowledge* and you don't *use* it! You don't look beyond school gossip, do you? Who got off together on Saturday night? Whose dad's buying a Porsche? And especially you guys, who claim to be keen on drama – you might at least *pretend* to take an interest, but you don't know what's happening at the end of the street, far less in the big wide world!'

We all stared at the floor. I sneaked a glance at Jimmy. He looked really angry, not as though he were acting.

'Come on, who, apart from William, Adrian and Morven, has actually heard of the Edinburgh Festival?'

Several hands went half up, including mine. I'd certainly heard of the festival but, like William, I thought it was something boring and highbrow.

Jimmy sighed. 'Well, people, for your information, whilst the greatest theatrical companies in the world are invited to the official festival, the Fringe is the *un*official festival. No-one invites you. You decide to go. There's nothing like it. It's the one place where anyone can perform – pros, amateurs, students, schoolkids – if you can scrape together the rent of a church hall and find a floor to sleep on. And then you're ready for fame and fortune – or bankruptcy.'

'You mean,' said William, 'it's like all those old movies where a bunch of kids want to put on a show and they haven't got a theatre, so someone says: "Let's do the show right here, in the old barn"?'

Jimmy gestured towards William, a long, graceful flourish. 'William, my hero. Not the clown he pretends to be, but the one person here who seems to know what I'm talking about.'

William leapt up and bowed, his crest of curly dark hair falling into his eyes.

'William is absolutely right. For three weeks, being in Edinburgh is exactly like being in an old movie. There is not a church or school or masonic hall but it has its troupe of wandering act*ors* engaged in that entrancing, magical activity known as "putting on a show".'

Jimmy's large dark eyes had lit up once more as he talked and performed his way back into a good temper. 'And next year, next year, my fellow thespians, I propose that we shall be among their number.'

A buzz of excitement had been building up during his last speech.

Jimmy held up his hand as people began to talk. 'I've discussed this with Mrs Jennings. Of course, if we decide to go ahead, we'll have to start fund-raising, and then we'll need to find a suitable venue, and accommodation – but the first thing is to make this show good enough to take to Edinburgh. Some of the young people's groups have been going for years and their standard is very,

very high. And there is no way I'm taking a show which isn't absolutely first-rate.'

You mean, there's no way you're going to be publicly connected with a failure, I thought sourly. Out loud I said: 'Will real newspaper critics come and see us?'

'If we're lucky. With literally hundreds of companies appearing, you can't be certain of a review – or an audience for that matter – but,' and he tapped the side of his nose, 'I have contacts.'

He is doing this for himself, I thought. He doesn't care about us. We're just – stepping stones in his career.

'But if there are so many companies taking part, what's the point?' said Morven disagreeably, drawing down the corners of her mean little mouth. No wonder she's not a better singer. There's no room in there for a decent note.

'The point! The point!' cried Jimmy, throwing his hands up into the air. 'If you don't get the point, I can't explain it to you. The excitement, the risk, the challenge – and even if you fail, you can always say: "Oh yeah, when I was on the Fringe . . ." ' He drawled the last few words in a broad, affected voice exactly like Randal's and we all laughed – even me.

Then he jumped to his feet. 'Come on, let's get this show on the road!'

I got up slowly, stifling my laughter. Jimmy might be infuriating, but he certainly had something. Personality? Charisma? But whatever it was, I wasn't going to let him charm *me*.

Chapter Five

When the rehearsal was over we all hung about the school gate. Everyone was excited by the idea of taking the show to Edinburgh.

'This could be a really big deal,' said William. 'You heard what Jimmy said – our names in lights—'

'He also said there are hundreds of companies,' pointed out Andy, who is William's sidekick and best friend. He goes around squashing William's optimistic ideas and generally trying to take him down – with no effect.

'Nah, Andy, it'll be cool. We'll be like a real theatre company, not just putting on a show for our parents.'

'Yes,' said Rachel, 'and it gives us a chance to say something politically relevant to a wider audience—'

'Come off it, Rachel, think what fun it'll be, that's what's really relevant,' said Dinah, shaking back her long, honey-coloured hair so that today's ear-rings, two little green snakes, slithered through the strands.

'But we're going to have to *get* a wider audience first,' stressed Adrian. 'First of all we've got to make the show good enough for Jimmy to agree to take us, and then, *if* we get to Edinburgh, we have to be good enough for strangers to pay money to come and see us.'

'But we *are* good enough,' said Dinah. Like William, she always expects the best.

'We look good here, but we don't know how we'll compare with other groups.'

'Well, Adrian, apart from any of the rest of us you're good, and so's Iris, and Jimmy's a brilliant director so we've got as good a chance of doing well as anyone.'

Several people looked at me as Dinah said my name.

'Yes, Iris, what do you think?' said Morven.

I knew that Morven wanted me to say that I thought it was a rotten idea and that I wasn't interested in going, because then she might get my part. But I wasn't giving up my specially composed songs to someone whose top notes are like those of a bat – inaudible.

'Well?' said Morven.

I hesitated. I'd made no secret of the fact that I disliked Jimmy and that I would've preferred to do a traditional show rather than an improvisation – but the news about Blake Evans had changed everything.

I swung my bag up onto my shoulder. 'I think we're *frightfully* lucky to have Jimmy,' I said, imitating him. 'And I think this show's going to be *terrific* – especially if we all work together and don't get involved in petty quarrels – *too* boring.'

Several people laughed and Morven stalked away, followed by Sarah, a boring girl whose main roles in life are being, one, a blonde, and two, Morven's best friend.

This broke the group up and we all went off in our various directions. Randal walked along behind Aly, Rachel and me.

'Well, Iris, you have changed your tune. I didn't

know you were quite so keen on us all working together, a jolly band of actors.'

'Oh, I was teasing Morven. But I do mean it. It would be fun to do a show actually in a festival.'

I spoke as casually as possible, but really, ever since Jimmy had mentioned the festival I had imagined seeing our show mentioned in the national press, with my own name prominent as a rising young star. Just a few lines – or maybe a lead review – perhaps a photo!

'It would be OK.' Randal was being irritatingly unexcited. 'But I think people are getting carried away. Even if Mrs Jennings and all our parents agree, it's going to be incredibly expensive – probably thousands of pounds for transport and renting a hall and a place to stay – and some people may have holiday plans and have to drop out.'

I hadn't thought of that. 'But *nothing* could be more important than doing a show!' I exclaimed.

Aly and Rachel both burst out laughing, to my annoyance.

'Oh, Iris, I knew you'd come round! You can't resist performing, can you?' Aly put her arm through mine.

'No, she can't resist having music written for her,' said Rachel.

'That's not fair,' cried Aly, sticking up for me as usual.

'Absolutely. We all know that without even trying, Iris is a shimmering, glowing star,' said Randal. And raising his hand to us, he turned off into the sidestreet where he lives and stalked away under the trees.

Somehow his mocking words seemed familiar, but it wasn't until I'd said goodnight to Aly and Rachel and was walking down the path between our neighbours' lighted windows and the cold, rustling shrubbery that I remembered where they came from – the musical *Singin' in the Rain*. And the character who describes herself as a shimmering star is actually the dumb blonde who has all the confidence in the world but none of the talent.

I stamped my way upstairs. I'd show Randal, I'd show Jimmy. I'd show everyone that I was more than just a pretty girl who could warble her way through a number. In this show I was going to act my socks off, as well as singing like a diva.

I strode into the kitchen. Maggie, for once, was at the stove, balanced on her high heels, with her *Observer* special offer genuine striped butcher's apron tied over her black skirt and white silk blouse. She was holding a garlic press (one of the famous gadgets) over a pan of simmering vegetables. It was obviously one of her rare mother's-in-the-kitchen days.

'The damn thing's not working,' she said, waving the garlic press. 'How can a thing this simple not work? Is there some secret which the French are keeping to themselves?'

Maggie spends quite a lot of time in France because she works for a firm which makes high street copies of *haute couture* clothes. However, despite this, her opinion of the French remains that of a suspicious Norfolk peasant. She may think she's got away from her background, but it keeps catching up with her.

Ignoring the garlic drama, I dropped my bag on the stripped and polished floor, and threw off my blazer and school scarf.

'Listen, Maggie, Jimmy's got this amazing plan that we should take the show to the Edinburgh Festival!'

Maggie suddenly gave up on the garlic. She slammed the press down on the worktop and, turning away from me, whipped up the contents of the pan with a wooden spoon. 'But I thought you weren't really interested in the play this year, darling.'

When she decides to cook, she really concentrates on the action. Now she was grinding pepper and tipping in chopped herbs. She didn't even look at me.

'Listen, I *told* you, you weren't listening, I *said* I'd decided to audition after all.'

'Well, that was nice of you. I know they'd have problems finding someone to take your place, but are you really going to have the time? You know this is a busy year for you academically.' She turned the heat up under the pan and a wall of steam rose between us. 'You know you have to work hard if you want to get into a good university.'

By a good university she means Oxford or Cambridge, not the redbrick where she got her business studies degree. Maggie took the first, web-footed step out of damp Norfolk and I'm supposed to take an even longer one into some awesomely famous hall of learning.

'But *listen* – ' I said, joining her in the cloud of steam.

She jammed a lid on the pan and clipped over to the sink. 'And I thought you said you weren't going to have a leading part this year. Surely in that case it would be better to give it up altogether rather than be a nobody in the chorus.'

She turned both taps on full, and the noise of the water striking the stainless steel reverberated around her.

The fact that she was saying exactly what I'd been

thinking a short while ago infuriated me. 'But it's not like that!' I shouted. 'Jimmy's friend Blake Evans the composer – he's going to be really famous some day, Jimmy says – well, he liked my voice so much that he's going to write something specially for *me*.'

Maggie washed her hands, turned off the taps, and reached for a towel. 'Really, Iris,' she said, walking away from me to fetch plates from the dresser, 'really, Iris, I don't think you should get too excited over this. This Jimmy is giving you all ridiculously big ideas. It's only a little school play.'

She put the plates on the table and lined up cutlery and glasses. She was really putting an unusual amount of energy into this Earth Mother routine.

'But I said we were going to the *Edinburgh Festival*! That won't be little. I'll be singing in front of a real audience, not just parents, and there may even be professional critics.'

My mother's eyes are as black as jet beads. Now she looked at me properly for the first time since I'd come into the room. 'Sometimes, Iris, I don't think you're ever going to grow up. All you think about is showing off and drawing attention to yourself. That's not going to get you very far in the real world.'

I put my hands on the back of a chair and leant towards her, speaking slowly and clearly. 'But if I want to go on the stage, these are exactly the qualities I need.'

'Going on the stage is a perfectly unrealistic notion,' she replied, with equal restraint.

'But it isn't. I've just told you. A professional composer is actually writing some songs for me.'

'A composer no-one's ever heard of, and songs in a show hardly anyone's going to see. I know that sounds harsh, but it's kinder to look at things the way they really are.'

We were bending towards each other over the table, eyes locked. And there was something in Maggie's gaze which disturbed me.

'Why are you so upset *now*?' I demanded. 'My parts in the other shows were far bigger and you didn't object to my doing them. What's different this year?'

Something in her face, in the way she glanced sideways and then back again, showed me that I was right. For once, my clever mother was confused.

'I've told you. A-levels. And the fact that all the attention is going to your head. You may be a big star here, but what would you be like compared to other people?'

'That's exactly what I want to find out. That's why I want to go to Edinburgh.'

'But how are you going to go to Edinburgh? When is the festival, August? I thought you were going to France with Rachel to stay with Jean-Paul's family?'

That shows how excited I was about the festival – I'd actually forgotten that I'd been going to see my old boyfriend!

'That wasn't a definite arrangement. And anyway, Rachel's in the show too.'

'But I thought you'd be longing to see Jean-Paul again!'

This was a weird thing for Maggie to say, because she had never liked Jean-Paul when we were going out together. ('He's not nearly as tall as Randal. But that's the French for you.')

'I can go to France again, but I may never have another chance to appear on the Fringe.'

Our argument had been accompanied by the bubbling of the famous home-made supper. Now we both became aware that the bubbling had changed to a dry, ominous frizzling sound. Maggie rushed to the stove, snatched the pan, and peered inside.

'Just in time. It'll taste more authentic. I tell you what, Iris' – she turned towards me, smiling brightly over our ruined supper – 'we could go to France together. Improve our cooking.'

I was so amazed that I plumped down on the nearest chair. We hadn't gone on holiday together since the days when we used to share some rat-infested cottage with Auntie Wyn and my dire cousins, Louise and Gerald. But now she was proposing that she and I, the mother and daughter least likely to maintain a civilized relationship, actually go and spend time together in France, where we'd be surrounded by the despised, French-speaking French people.

'You don't seem very pleased. I thought you'd like the idea.' Maggie spooned the burnt ratatouille onto our plates, and added slices of baguette, which had been charring in the oven.

'I'm just surprised. I thought you and Auntie Wyn were going to Turkey. Sun, sand, and whirling dervishes.'

'But it's so long since you and I did anything together.' Maggie sat down opposite me and began eating with a great air of enthusiasm.

Well, the reason for that is that you and I don't get on well enough to *want* to do anything together, I thought. We're simply being realistic by spending as little time together as possible.

I was suddenly seized by painful memories of the time when things had been different – painful because that time seemed so distant. When I was little, I used to wait eagerly for Maggie to come home from work. She'd take over from Heidi, my nanny, giving me my bath and then reading to me in bed. I'd beg her to tell me stories about growing up on the farm, or about the fun which she and Auntie Wyn had when they shared a flat in Camden Town. But as I grew older, these good times together became less frequent. I could bath myself. I was too old to be read to. Maggie was promoted, and as her work grew more demanding, she began to expect more of me. Her pride in my juvenile achievements was gradually transformed into a determination that I succeed as she had done. We were to be the mother and daughter team who had made good.

Now we ate silently in the fashionable and expensive kitchen which Maggie's hard work had won for us.

After a while Maggie said: 'Well, darling, you can always think about it. Our going away together.'

'OK,' I replied coldly. 'I can always think.'

Chapter Six

'It's so bizarre, she hasn't wanted us to go away together since I was about *eleven.*'

It was the next day, after school, and Aly and I were sitting on the floor in the pool of light thrown by her bedside lamp. We were drinking herb tea and eating sunflower seeds, a typical snack for the austere Bywaters household. Whales and dolphins cavorted on posters in the shadows above us, and outside it was dark and wet. We could've been alone together at the bottom of the sea.

'Perhaps that's why she wants to go with you now.'

I picked at a loose tuft in the rag rug. The idea made me very uncomfortable. 'But we just don't get on. You know that.'

'Well, I expect she knows it too, and she wants to do better.'

This is the sort of exasperating, optimistic view which Aly always takes of people.

'People aren't always as nice as you think they are,' I said. 'No, if she really wanted to be a better parent she'd try to *understand* why this show is so important to me, but she won't *listen*. She just goes on about A-levels. I can work night and day, it doesn't matter how much I do, or how well I do it, it's still never enough.'

'But everyone wants their kids to do well.'

'But not everyone is obsessed with it like she is.'

'I suppose she feels like that because you're all she's got.'

This made me feel worse than ever, as though I had to be responsible for Maggie's happiness for the rest of my life. I exploded at Aly. 'She's got nobody to blame but herself! Why didn't my father stay with her? I bet she bullied him too until he'd had enough and took off.'

'Oh, Iris, you don't know that's what happened! Perhaps he was married already. Or perhaps she didn't *want* him to stay.'

'Oh, how do I know? She still won't tell me about him.'

I leant against the bed and stared out at the falling rain. I don't even know my father's name. Nothing at all – age, nationality, where they met, whether they'd been in love. Last time I'd asked, she'd said: 'Just a little romance, something you'll understand when you're older.' Well, I *was* older, but apparently never old enough.

'There's one thing, though,' I said, breaking the silence which had fallen between us. 'I bet I *look* like him.' No-one else in Maggie's family is tall and slim with chestnut hair and navy-blue eyes.

I glanced over at Aly. She was watching me with such sympathy that I suddenly felt like crying. 'What I don't understand,' I said quickly, 'is why Maggie's so dead set against my going to Edinburgh. I mean, the festival's in August, that's not going to interfere with work.'

'Maybe she'd already planned this holiday with you as a surprise.'

'Oh, Aly, stop being so *nice*! Maggie *hates* going away with me! It's the last thing she would want to do!'

'Honestly, you just have this really bad opinion of your mother without ever finding out what she really thinks. You're just as bad as she is.'

'But I do know what she thinks! She thinks I should give up my career!'

'Singing's hardly your career yet.'

For a moment it looked as though we were going to quarrel for the second time in a few days. I couldn't bear it. I had to have Aly's support. 'Come on, Aly,' I said, 'don't look so stern. It's this show, it's making me all twitchy, it's so different from anything we've done before.'

Aly's face had taken on a prim expression, but she relaxed when I spoke. 'I'm sorry, Iris, I know it's important to you. It's just, well, singing isn't everything.' She gestured at the Greenpeace and World Wildlife posters which swam above us in the lamplit room.

'You're as bad as Rachel!' I said. 'Tell you what, when I'm famous, I'll do a big concert for the charity of your choice.'

'That'll be the day.'

We laughed, but I couldn't help reverting to our original subject.

'No, but the thing is, Maggie doesn't want me to do the festival. She got really peculiar when it came up – as though something about it really upset her.'

'But the difference is that this time you're really serious. I mean, before she could always say to herself that it was just the school show, but now it's less easy for her to write it off.'

I considered Aly's words. 'I suppose you're right.' What she said made sense, but I couldn't forget the glimpse of something which I'd seen in Maggie's face as we looked at one another over the table. The words that came into my head were 'panic-stricken'.

By the time I left it was dark. It was still pouring, but Aly's mother had insisted upon lending me an umbrella. As I approached our house, enjoying the sensation of being dry amidst so much wet, I saw a car outside which I recognized at once, despite the gloom. Wyn's Renault. Acting on impulse, I avoided the gravel and approached the house across the soggy grass. I tiptoed up the stairs and very, very carefully turned my key in the lock. Then I pushed open the door. Sure enough, I could hear voices in the sitting room. The umbrella fluttered and thumped like a huge bird as I tried to fold it silently. I put it down with my bag, where they dripped together on the hall floor, and then untied and removed my boots. At last I was ready to creep down the hall, from one rug to the next, and, reaching the door, I bent down and listened.

I could hear Maggie's voice clearly. 'Honestly, Wyn, I'm at my wit's end. I thought she would've grown out of this nonsense by now.'

Wyn's reply was inaudible.

Maggie said: 'Yes, I know I can't stop her for *ever*. I just got such a shock when she said "Edinburgh" – and besides I feel this is a very bad time. She needs stability just now, peace and quiet to get on with her work.'

Wyn's response was again too quiet for me to hear, but Maggie, far removed from her usual calm, was almost shouting. 'I hardly think "paranoid" is the appropriate term! I'm not being paranoid about this, simply realistic.'

Wyn raised her voice slightly. 'But Maggie, you know you can't keep her as your little girl for ever. She's got to grow up, whether you like it or not.'

'I'm hardly so unnatural as to object to her

growing, for heaven's sake, Wyn! What I object to is all this happening now.'

Wyn said: 'But you knew that this was bound to happen some day.'

Maggie's words cut back at her. 'Not necessarily so. Not necessarily so at all. Until now, Iris has always done what I wanted.'

I drew back from the door. I suddenly felt cold in my stocking soles and damp blazer. So I always did what Maggie wanted! Was that really how she saw me – meek, obedient little Iris? Anger and resentment rose through my body from my cold feet to the crown of my head. Not this time, I told myself. Not this time. I'm going to sing in the show *and* I'm going to Edinburgh. She can't stop me. I'm going to be so brilliant that Jimmy'll *insist* that I go!

I imagined Jimmy facing Maggie. 'It's *imperative* that Iris come with us,' he would say, raising his long, slim hands in one of his eloquent gestures. 'We can't do the show without her, it's as simple as that.'

'But there must be an understudy,' Maggie would quaver weakly.

'Oh, someone else could play that part – but only Iris can *live* it!'

Yes, that's what I'd do. I'd make myself *indispensable*. Feeling triumphant already, I gathered up my bag and padded into the kitchen.

By the time Maggie and Wyn emerged from the sitting room, Maggie carrying their glasses and an empty wine bottle, I was demurely nibbling a microwaved snack.

'Iris! Haven't seen you for ages. Working hard?' My aunt was surveying me closely, presumably for signs of the nonsense out of which I hadn't grown.

Wyn, who sells advertising for an upmarket

women's magazine, is what she herself calls a 'creative dresser'. Today she was wearing a giant purple-and-green striped shawl swathed over her little black dress, and ear-rings made out of silver nuts and bolts. She now went through a performance of removing the shawl, putting on a long black coat, and rearranging the shawl around her shoulders. Then she donned a large, flat velvet hat, trimmed with purple ribbon. As Wyn is no taller than Maggie, although much slimmer, she ended up resembling a little old evil fairy, the sort who ask impossible riddles or set impossible tasks.

'I barely see Louise and Gerry these days,' she went on, as she patted and tweaked herself into place. 'They're both upstairs in their rooms, working, working, working. Of course, Gerry's already got an acceptance for next year, but he thought he'd like to add Latin to his repertoire.'

I smiled politely.

'And Lou doesn't like to be left behind.'

It wasn't difficult to smile again, as Louise, although an academic whizz, is very obviously never going to have an acceptable boyfriend.

'And I've got good news too,' I said, looking up from my instant lasagne. 'Did Maggie tell you that Blake Evans, the composer, is writing a couple of songs for me?'

Maggie sighed and made a what-did-I-tell-you gesture.

'Yes,' I continued cheerfully. 'He's writing the music for this year's show, and he seemed to really like my voice. He's going to write for my upper register as I'm the only one in the cast who can really reach the top notes without straining.'

This was a small lie – not about my top notes, as I'm easily the best soprano in the group – but about Blake writing something which only I could sing. However, it was all part of my plan. Let Maggie think that I'd be letting everyone down if I didn't go to Edinburgh.

'And of course, I don't let my music interfere with my work.' I smiled sweetly as I picked up the French book which I had laid ostentatiously beside my plate. 'Not even meals stop this little student.'

'Darling Iris, still set upon being a star!'

Wyn tapped across the kitchen in her tiny, high-heeled boots and kissed me on both cheeks. Then she tapped across to Maggie and they enacted a mutual embrace, carefully avoiding the velvet hat.

'Phone me,' said Wyn, tucking in some hennaed curls. She added, in a melodramatic whisper: 'Keep me *abreast*.'

Maggie ushered her out and along the hall, where they had a last bout of conspiracy. I didn't bother to listen. I was planning ahead.

Chapter Seven

My plans, however, hadn't taken Jimmy's attitude into account. I'd assumed that once I got into my part he'd stop complaining about my work and begin behaving like the fantasy Jimmy who'd insisted to Maggie that I couldn't leave the show because I was the undisputed star. The real-life Jimmy had a completely different idea of my abilities. The rehearsals became a repeat of the day when I'd died so gracefully and movingly – and Jimmy had ranted about my overdoing the emotion. As though one could overdo *dying*.

My character in the show, based upon Janine's idea, was a young married woman named Effie, who is pregnant for the first time. In those days, Rachel told us, women were incredibly innocent, and knew absolutely nothing about childbirth until it happened to them. So Effie's ignorance adds to her fear. In my first scene I'm having tea with Mrs Simpson and two friends in her Edinburgh drawing room. They are all older than Effie and already have children, so they're enjoying a gossip about their experiences during labour, not noticing that I'm horrified by their conversation. Then I get up and sing my big number about being unable to reveal my feelings to my family because they're all so excited about the baby. It's a heart-stopping, dramatic moment.

However, Jimmy kept ruining it by insisting that we rehearse again and again until I'd no feeling left to bring to the scene.

One day, about two weeks into rehearsals, I felt that I'd gone completely flat. I'd been up late the night before doing a French essay – I couldn't let my studies slip – and it seemed absolutely the last straw to have to go over the tea-party scene yet again. But, to my surprise, Jimmy seemed to be quite pleased.

'We're getting there,' he announced. 'Aly and Morven, you're picking up on your cues nice and fast, no untidy gaps. Good, Dinah.'

I waited for the usual moans about my work.

'Hmmm, Iris,' he said.

I looked straight back at him.

'Much better.'

At last! But how could I possibly be acting better when I was too tired to try?

'Much quieter, that's what I want. And you refrained from twitching and starting all over the place like a frightened horse. Keep it up – or keep it down, rather.'

I was too astonished to reply. Jimmy was praising my worst performance ever!

'Right – we'll go on from Janine's entrance.'

Janine, playing the part of the Simpsons' daughter, Jessie, ran on to say that her father, the doctor, was asleep in his study and she couldn't rouse him. Of course, he's been experimenting with chloroform and put himself to sleep. The ladies don't know this, and flutter out in alarm.

Even I had to admit that Janine acted her part very well. She was also the only one of us, apart from Adrian as Dr Simpson, who could manage a convincing Scottish accent.

'Excellent,' said Jimmy, when we'd finished. 'Janine, I like the way you manage to be funny as well as alarmed. You're really building a nice little character there. It's a pity your voice isn't stronger or we could've given you a song.'

Well, that was something to be thankful for. A Janine who could suddenly sing as well as act would be too much to cope with.

Janine was listening to Jimmy, looking annoyingly wistful, like a puppy longing to please its master.

Watching her reminded me that I hadn't done much to fulfil the resolution I'd made of being nicer to her. After both Aly and Randal had gone on at me for making her play my daughter in the death scene, I'd decided to make up for my tactlessness by being extra friendly. That would show Randal that I wasn't the selfish, big-headed person he thought I was.

It's difficult, however, being nice to someone who scuttles away from you in terror, which is what Janine always does. But I don't give up easily, so once I'd decided to be charming, nothing was going to stop me.

Now, seeing Randal coming towards us, I quickly said the first thing that came into my head. 'That's a great-looking bag. Is it new?'

Janine, who was putting away her script, looked up in surprise.

The bag was actually very unusual. It was a large satchel made out of old, thick, rose-patterned velvet.

For once, Janine didn't turn and run. 'It is pretty, isn't it?' She spoke without quite meeting my eye. 'I bought it in Camden Market, last Saturday. Aly helped me choose it.'

Aly! My friend Alabama had gone to Camden

Market with weasely little Janine and never told me! And on Saturday, which was *our* day for going shopping together.

I would've been speechless, but I was determined not to show my surprise, especially as Randal was now standing beside us. 'Oh, so that's the bag?' I said casually. 'I thought it was smaller from the way she described it.'

And I smiled and strolled away.

As I left I heard Randal say: 'Look, Janine, do you think we could get together and rehearse our scene some time?'

I just couldn't believe what Janine had said. Surely Aly wouldn't go to the market with her?

I thought back to last Saturday. Aly had been collecting for Amnesty with her mother, and in the afternoon I'd had a singing lesson. Mr Stoller, my new teacher, had swapped the times around because one of his professional pupils needed an emergency lesson before an audition. So Aly and Janine could've gone out together.

I snatched up my stuff and hurried outside.

Aly was waiting for me at the gate. 'C'mon, Iris,' she said, bobbing up and down and hugging her arms across her chest. 'It's too cold to hang about.'

She was wearing a big navy jacket with the collar turned up to her ears.

'And where's Randal? I'm not going to wait for him, even if he does complain about being left behind.'

'He's talking to *Janine*,' I said nastily, sweeping past her. 'There's no point in waiting.'

'All right. I said I was cold, I didn't say we had to run.'

I was striding away from the school as quickly as possible. 'You never told me you'd gone to Camden

Market with Janine on Saturday,' I said, over my shoulder.

Aly didn't reply, so I turned round to look at her.

'Well?' I said.

'Because I knew you'd be like this.'

'Like what?'

'Making a fuss.'

'Oh yeah? So that's what this is, is it? A fuss? When you arrange to go out with Janine, of all people, you say I'm making a fuss! Well, it's a lot bigger than a fuss!'

'But I didn't *arrange* to go out with her! And anyway, she's perfectly nice when you get to know her.'

'Well, what do you think I was doing today? I was getting to know her, and she tells me that you helped her choose her new bag on Saturday, when you told me you'd be selling flags with your mum.'

'But that was only in the morning! In the afternoon I went down to Camden Lock by myself because you were at your lesson, and I ran into Janine by accident. I hadn't arranged to meet her or anything.'

'Huh.' I began to walk on.

'Honestly, Iris, do you really think I'd go shopping with Janine in secret?'

'But you didn't tell me about it, so if that's not a secret, what is?'

'I should have. I should have told you.'

I could hear that Aly was blaming herself, something which she is very inclined to do. I mean, she already blames herself for the plight of whales, dolphins and political prisoners, so I dare say that betraying her best friend wouldn't add much to her burden of guilt.

'I meant to tell you I'd met her, but I knew you'd

be horrible about it because you despise Janine so much. I mean, you're not exactly sisterly towards her, are you?'

I was taken aback by Aly's fierce words. I may think Janine's a bit wimpish and unattractive, but that's not the same as despising her.

'Well, why should I be? You're sounding just like Rachel. Janine Boswell isn't my sister.'

'I just meant, she's in our group, and she's unhappy, so you might be a bit nicer to her.'

'Well,' I said, 'if you think I'm so awful, I'm not surprised you don't want to go out with me.'

'I didn't say that.'

'Yes, you did. You said I was horrible and that I go round despising people.'

'I did not say you were horrible. I said you could be horrible. That's different. And you do despise people – not just Janine. I mean, you're always saying how Morven can't sing and Sarah's a dumb blonde and Dinah doesn't think and Rachel thinks too much – when did you last say something *nice* about someone?'

We were both shocked into silence by Aly's outburst. Without realizing it, we'd reached my gate and I'd automatically put my hand on the latch. I looked at Aly. The colour had been bleached out of her face by the streetlights, but I guessed that she was bright pink with anger.

'Well, thank you very much for giving me your opinion,' I said, opening the gate. 'I'll know better in future than to expect you to go anywhere with me.' And I turned my back on Aly and marched up the path. I sneaked a look behind me as I turned the corner of the house, but she had already gone.

* * *

I half-expected Aly to phone all evening. We hadn't had a real fight since we were in primary school and I was jealous because she was chosen to be the Christmas fairy. It seemed impossible that we were quarrelling now – and over Janine, whom no-one had even noticed until Jimmy gave her a part. It was all his fault! Why did he have to come and upset things? We'd all been perfectly happy when Miss Kerr was in charge.

I went to bed early so that I could brood under the duvet. If only I could be ill the next day and not have to go to school. Then no-one would see that Aly and I weren't speaking. I couldn't bear to think of people gossiping about us. But if Aly didn't make up, did that mean that I had to? Certainly not! I hadn't done anything wrong. I wasn't the one who'd gone sneaking around behind her best friend's back. It was Aly, stuck-up and goody-goody, who was in the wrong.

However, when I set out next morning, I found Aly waiting on the corner as usual. I was so relieved to see her that I almost felt ready to apologize, but I walked up to her slowly in case she was ready to say she was sorry first.

She was. 'Hello, Iris,' she said. 'I'm sorry if I hurt your feelings yesterday.'

I felt ready to be generous. 'Oh, that's all right.' We Leos are very forgiving when we're asked nicely.

'I mean, I *am* sorry I hurt your feelings but I'm not sorry I went shopping with Janine.' Aly's voice was unusually cold and sharp.

I began to stroll towards school. A tight, suffocating pain was starting to build up in my chest.

'I said it was all right. I said yesterday we didn't always have to go out together.'

I expected Aly to say something friendly like 'Don't be silly,' or 'You know I'd rather do things with you than with anyone else.' But she didn't. Instead we walked on in silence.

I began to feel more and more uncomfortable. I glanced at Aly. She was staring straight ahead, pale and stern. I guessed that I had come up against her conscience, her conscience which makes her release hamsters and save whales and sell flags. If she thought that befriending lonely Janine was the right thing to do then she would do it, and not even I would be able to stop her. But after all, I'd still be her *best* friend.

'I mean it,' I said. 'Really, Aly. Go to the market again with Janine if you want to.'

Aly turned towards me, starting to smile. 'We could all go together.'

'No way!' I exclaimed. I wasn't going to waste a whole afternoon being nice. Ten minutes was about my limit. 'I mean, Janine always behaves as though she were terrified of me. She probably wouldn't come if I were there.'

'OK.' Aly accepted this without argument. 'I'll ask her next time you've got a lesson on Saturday.'

'It's a deal.' I grinned. As I don't often have lessons on Saturday, it was a small sacrifice to make for Aly's good opinion.

By the time we reached school we were chatting almost normally, and the tightness in my chest and throat had relaxed. No-one seeing us could've guessed that the unthinkable had happened. Inseparable Iris and Alabama had quarrelled.

Chapter Eight

Then, as Dinah, who is very into New Age philosophy, would've said, fate took a hand. Or perhaps the Law of Karma came into effect.

Anyway, that evening Mr Stoller phoned. He wanted to change my lessons to Saturday afternoons. 'If you come at two-thirty, I can give you a whole hour,' he said cheerfully.

Well, Mr Stoller is a very busy and respected teacher, so I could hardly say, sorry, I don't want a lesson on Saturdays, I'd rather go out with my friends. Especially as he was offering me an hour instead of the three-quarters I had at present.

So I sighed, but said as enthusiastically as possible: 'Thank you, that'll be really great.'

'Now, I know what you young girls are like,' he continued, almost as though he could uncannily read my mind over the phone. 'You like to wander round the shops and drink coffee on Saturday afternoons. So I'm happy to tell you that I can let you off every fourth week, when I've got a pupil coming from out of town.'

'That'll be ideal, then, thank you,' I said, suddenly realizing with horror that I was sounding exactly like Maggie when she discusses business.

Mr Stoller chuckled merrily and rang off, and I slumped into the rocking chair. So from now on Aly could do anything she liked on Saturday afternoons because I'd be trilling away in Hampstead. I wondered if I'd caused this to happen by saying that I never expected her to go out with me again. I mean, could some psychic wave of invisible badness have gone swooshing from me to Mr Stoller and caused him to change my lesson? It didn't seem very likely, but perhaps I'd better watch what I said from now on.

At two-thirty on Saturday I pressed Mr Stoller's bell and he buzzed me in. When I'd told Aly about the new lesson times she'd said she'd meet me afterwards in Hampstead High Street, so I was feeling quite cheerful as I went up the stairs of the converted house and opened the heavy door to Mr Steller's flat. The previous pupil was still there, as I could tell from the piano scales which came booming out from behind the studio door. I say 'piano' because I could hardly hear the thin, tentative voice which went with it.

I grinned to myself. Obviously some beginner.

I went on down the hall, between the huge pieces of dark, carved furniture, intending to hang my coat on the curly stand at the far end. But a jacket, woolly hat and bag were already hanging there. A bag which I recognized with a curious lack of surprise. Rose-patterned velvet.

So that's what was in Janine's head when Jimmy told her that her voice wasn't strong enough for a song, and she was looking so wistful. She had decided to learn to sing! And she'd chosen *my* teacher because I'd been stupid enough to waffle on about how marvellous he was. At least, judging by the sounds which were coming through the door, learning was going to take a long time. But I'd underestimated Janine. She obviously had more character than I'd ever given her credit for. Just wait until I told Aly! But if I told her, she'd probably approve of Janine even more than she seemed to do at present. No, it would definitely be a bad idea. Let Janine tell Aly herself if they were such friends.

I suddenly realized that the music had stopped and that Mr Stoller was moving towards the hall. I ducked into the bathroom and listened behind the door while he ushered Janine out.

'Exercises every day! Vital!'

I noisily ran some water into the basin and washed my hands. Then I emerged as Mr Stoller came back down the hall.

'There you are, Iris! Come on, down to work, not a moment to lose.'

Mr Stoller has a lot of grey hair combed straight back from his brow, and a face which must once have been noble and craggy, but is now wrinkled and creased. He always wears the same old-fashioned clothes: corduroy trousers, a plain Viyella shirt and a velvet waistcoat, but manages to look trim and artistic rather than stuffy.

I followed him into the studio, which is full of more gloomy furniture, arranged on a dark-red carpet, with the huge grand piano in the middle.

I took out my new song and handed it to Mr Stoller. We'd already been working on my tea-party song, and on my verse of the final number, which is when all the women line up in costumes from Victorian days to the present and sing 'Hail, Anaesthesia!' and the men then come and join in. But Blake had only just finished my second solo, a lullaby set to his version of an old Scottish tune.

Mr Stoller took the music and glanced through it. 'Hmm, hmm, I like what this young man is doing. Right. Let's get warmed up.'

And we embarked upon my arpeggios.

Mr Stoller is very strict and, like Jimmy, sometimes says really unkind things to me – once he told me that if I weren't careful I'd turn into a 'swooning soprano', a singer with awful, syrupy top notes. But I don't mind what he says because, *un*like Jimmy, I feel that he respects my talent and only wants me to work hard so that I don't waste it.

'*Bel-la sign-or-a!*'

I sang the exercise up and down the scales, going higher and higher, listening to my voice ringing out. If anyone had been in the hall, they would definitely have heard *my* voice over the piano.

I stayed true to my resolution and didn't mention Janine's lessons to Aly. In fact, I never saw her there again, and I wondered if she'd asked for a different time so's not to meet me. Perhaps she was afraid I'd make fun of her efforts.

Anyway, she seemed to be avoiding me totally. If Aly and I were talking, and Aly tried to include her, Janine would make some excuse and scuttle away. And if, as had happened once or twice, I found Aly and Janine together, Janine would disappear at my approach. I decided that she had guessed I was angry about the Camden Market affair and was hiding from me. But I wasn't going to let her see I was upset. Let Janine and Aly go to all the markets in London, what did I care?

Of course, I did care quite a lot, especially as, after the Saturday when Aly met me after my lesson, she'd made other plans for the afternoons. The first time, Janine had invited her round for tea, and the second, she and Janine had gone into town to buy a nightie for Janine's mother, who was going back into hospital. But the next Saturday was my day off, when Mr Stoller had another pupil, so I was determined that Aly and I would get together.

I'd been trying to find Aly all day, but it was beginning to feel as though she, like Janine, was avoiding me. However, I knew I'd see her at rehearsal – and there she was, sitting on a bench in the wings with Janine and Dinah. As we were now only ten days away from opening night, we were rehearsing on stage with some of the set and props, so the girls were wearing tatty old tulle petticoats over their navy school skirts – Jimmy likes us to rehearse in long skirts to get the 'feel' of period costume – and, sitting together, they looked like one of the ballet pictures I used to have up in my room when I was little. Aly and Dinah were leaning towards Janine, looking concerned and sorrowful, while Janine, I now realized, was crying into a crumpled pink tissue.

Pathetic little waterspout, I thought. And then I remembered her mother. I moved closer, keeping behind Dr Simpson's painted canvas bookshelf.

'Oh, Janine, I am sorry,' Aly was saying.

Sniffle sniffle sniffle, went Janine.

'Perhaps she'll be able to come up to Edinburgh and see the show there,' said Dinah.

Janine shook her head, her straggly hair brushing over her thin shoulders.

'C'mon, everybody, this is a rehearsal, for God's sake!' Jimmy was standing centre stage and shouting. He saw the mournful group and strode towards them. 'Janine, you're meant to be onstage. Randal, for once, is on time, so why aren't you?'

Sure enough, behind Jimmy I could see Randal, sitting on a tiny, button-backed chair, his legs sprawled out across the stage. He, too, was now looking towards the girls.

'What's happening?' continued Jimmy. 'You know my rule: no tears until after the last night. Until then nobody cries but me.'

Aha, I thought, the teacher's pet was getting into trouble at last. Let her see what it felt like.

Aly stood up. 'Janine's upset because her mother's going to miss the show. She has to go into hospital earlier than she expected.'

The anger faded from Jimmy's face. He sat down beside Janine and put his arm round her. I felt a thrill of exasperation. Why was he wasting so much time on a crybaby? Would I have to start crying if I wanted Jimmy's good opinion? No way!

'That's very hard luck,' he was saying gently, 'but I'm afraid that when these things happen, there's nothing to do but behave as professionally as possible.'

'You mean, the show must go on?' said Janine feebly, looking at Jimmy with tear-swollen, adoring eyes.

I *was* sorry for Janine, but this scene was totally over the top.

Jimmy may have thought so too, because he said, 'Absolutely,' quite briskly, and removed his arm from her shoulders. 'Now there's something I want to suggest to you.'

Janine nodded eagerly, mopping up her face with the soggy tissue.

Jimmy could certainly choose the right moment – if he told her he'd decided to cut her best scene she'd probably agree. However, he wanted something much less drastic. 'It's your hair,' he said. 'It's too long.'

Totally correct, I agreed silently. Janine's hair is the sort of limp brown seaweedy stuff which should never be allowed to grow beyond shoulder length.

'Too long for your part,' he continued swiftly, as Janine began to look surprised, and even slightly offended. 'I think that, as a little Victorian girl, you should have ringlets, but the weight of your hair would pull them out of curl. Sarah, you look like a beauty expert, what do you think?'

Sarah, who had been drawn to our little corner by the drama, looked pleased and important. She touched her own expensively blond locks.

'Mmm,' she said, considering Janine with a professional air. 'If you had about three inches trimmed off, you could set it on really big rollers and then use ultra-hold to keep the ringlets in place.'

'And what about a light perm?' suggested Aly. 'That would give it more body.'

'But not the crinkly sort,' said Dinah.

The three girls were really getting into this, clustering round Janine and holding up strands of her hair. Janine was perking up under all the attention. 'I'll get it done on Saturday afternoon,' she said, 'and then I'll have plenty of time to try out the ringlets before Thursday.'

Thursday was the first night. We were performing Thursday, Friday, and twice on Saturday.

'Great. I'll come with you,' said Aly.

Aly had forgotten that this Saturday was my day without a lesson! I began to feel tight and painful inside, as I had when we first quarrelled. But I wouldn't let anyone know how I felt. I backed away into the dark wings as Randal approached the group from the stage.

'Aren't we going to start soon? Even I can't lounge around for ever. What are you all doing?'

'Janine's hairstyle,' said Jimmy. 'We're discussing how to make her sufficiently sweet and Victorian.'

'Janine, you are already sufficiently sweet and Victorian for me,' drawled Randal, taking her hand and pulling her up.

I listened in amazement. Was he joking? My friend Randal? I couldn't tell.

Chapter Nine

So things weren't going well. I'd been looking forward so much to doing a new show and now nothing was turning out as I'd expected. Despite my two songs, I didn't have a big starring role, as Jimmy had insisted that the good parts be divided out evenly. He was still nagging me about my acting, and Maggie was nagging me about my work. And worst of all, although Aly and I still spent a lot of time together, our relationship had somehow altered. It was as though I'd taken off a comfy old pair of boots and were now tottering around in high heels, having to be very careful and balanced with every step. I felt that if I said or did the wrong thing, our awful quarrel would break out all over again and she'd look at me in that cold, angry way and tell me what an unpleasant person I was.

But luckily I was too busy to brood. Rehearsals, costume-fitting, and scenery-painting were taking up the last days of term, and everyone was becoming hyper and frantic. Even Jimmy.

'Where the hell are my notes?' he wailed.

We had just finished the last rehearsal before the dress, and he'd got us all together for a final pep-talk.

'I had them in my hand! Did I put them down somewhere? Or did I go mad and put them back in my bag?'

'I think you *did* put them back, Jimmy,' said Janine, who was sitting on the floor beside Randal. Every so often she would give her head a little toss, as though for the pleasure of feeling her hair settle back in soft tendrils around her face.

I had to admit that the new style improved her looks. The weight of curls at the back of her head balanced her nose and made it appear shorter. And although she looked even paler and more anxious since her mother had returned to hospital, there also seemed to be a new sparkle and energy about her.

'Did I, Janine?' said Jimmy, glancing at her. He had already admired her hair excessively when she came in on Monday, but perhaps he couldn't resist another look. I shook my own red hair impatiently. *I* never needed a perm or a tint to improve my looks!

'Notes, are you in there?'

Jimmy picked up his battered leather bag and shook out the contents. Pens, scripts, books, a set of juggling balls, a bottle of spring water, a handful of orange peel, all skidded across the floor. One of the books, a small paperback, landed at William's feet.

'Is this really yours, Jimmy?' he said, holding it up so that we could all see it. 'Absolutely, definitely your property?'

Intrigued by William's tone, we all stared at the book, first in disbelief, and then in amazement.

The book, decorated with a photo of a plump, naked infant, was entitled *Naming Your Baby*.

'When's the happy event?' continued William, grinning.

Jimmy groaned and buried his head in his folded arms. Then he emerged and said: 'Not until April, but it's such a *challenge*, finding the totally correct name, that one has to start the search well in advance.'

'You mean, you're really having a baby?' said Dinah, her voice squeaky with surprise. As usual, she was the first person to manage to say something.

'Well, not me personally. My wife is actually *having* the baby, but I dare say I'll be involved.'

We all continued to stare at him. It was somehow very hard to imagine Jimmy, whom we'd come to regard as our property, as a husband and father.

Then Rachel spoke up. 'I hope you're going to childbirth classes with your wife,' she said severely. 'And you will be present at the birth.'

'Oh yes, miss,' said Jimmy, 'unless I've got a first night.'

Rachel's eyes and mouth went wide with horror.

'No, no, joke!' said Jimmy hastily before she could express her outrage. 'Of course I'll be there.'

'Perhaps you'll faint,' said William hopefully.

'Now, Jimmy,' said Dinah seriously, 'listen, because this is very important. You must write down the exact moment that the baby is born, so you can get a birth chart drawn up.'

Astrology is one of Dinah's hobbies. When she gets going she's as bad as Rachel on social injustice.

'In fact,' she continued, 'I'll do it myself. It'll be my present to the baby.'

'Dinah, that would be wonderful,' said Jimmy, looking really pleased. 'Tilda was just saying that we'd have to get the baby's horoscope.'

Tilda. His wife's name was Tilda. Jimmy was *married* to a woman named Tilda who was about to have his baby. Not that I cared, of course. I mean, I hated Jimmy! Look at all the ghastly, insulting things he'd said about me. And the way he'd made fun of darling *Sound of Music*. Perhaps once he was a father he'd grow up a bit and be less childish and obnoxious.

Everyone was now crowding round him and asking questions and offering advice like a bunch of grannies and grandpas. Would he be disappointed if the baby didn't grow up to be an actor? Was his wife going to breastfeed? Was he making sure that she got enough sleep?

While I listened, a curious, empty feeling grew inside me. Jimmy was laughing as he replied patiently to all the daffy queries. He was obviously enjoying himself, stroking his pony-tail, waving his hands, acting the role of an expectant father. I ought to have been irritated, but I suddenly realized why I felt empty. I had lost my anger. I hadn't felt really angry with Jimmy for days. When I had said I hated him, it was simply from habit. I didn't hate him because I was in love with him. I was a silly girl with a silly crush on a teacher. A *married* teacher. How childish and humiliating and *stupid*. But at least no-one *knew*. Thank goodness everyone thought I loathed him. So that's what I'd do. I'd pretend, even to myself, that I'd never wanted him to admire me or touch me or put his arm around my shoulders as he had with Janine.

It wouldn't be so difficult. After all, I was an actress.

I took a deep breath. The terrible empty feeling was spreading inside me. My chest was a huge aching cavity. My whole body felt raw and painful and unwanted. Aly was no longer my best friend. Maggie didn't seem to love me. Jimmy was married and about to have a baby. This baby would know her father's name and how he looked and smelt and sounded. Not like me.

I knew that I was going to cry, in the same awful,

cold, certain way you know you're going to be sick. Very quietly I picked up my things and crept out of the hall.

No-one noticed. William had opened the book and was reading out the more outlandish names, while the others made even weirder suggestions.

'Wolfsbane would be so cool.'

'Nah, just call it Fang.'

'Cinnamon Rose for a girl.'

'Yuk.'

I ran down the stairs, racing my tears. If I could just get out into the dark before they started . . . the tears won, but as it was after school hours no-one saw me stumbling out the door, pink and blotchy and sobbing.

I ran all the way home, and then went straight to my room and threw myself on the bed. Luckily Maggie was at an office party, so I could sob as loudly as I liked.

The worst of it was, I felt so angry with *myself*. How could I fall in love with someone as exasperating and horrible as Jimmy? Someone who never even looked at me? Someone who was *married*?

I rolled over onto my stomach and howled into the duvet. This wasn't the behaviour I expected from Iris Campion.

'What happened to you last night? Why did you leave so early?'

Aly and I were in the wings, waiting for the dress rehearsal to start. She was wearing a dark-blue crinoline and shawl with a white collar and cap, while I wore a beautiful pale lilac dress and a real lace shawl lent by someone's granny. All around us the stage crew were moving scenery or fixing lights, despite Jimmy yelling that they ought to have finished hours ago.

He was standing in the middle of the chaos, brandishing his clipboard, all in black, lithe as a panther – I was horrified to find myself thinking like this! It was so humiliating. What if I began saying these things out loud?

I made myself listen to Aly.

'He was really furious, but I said you weren't feeling well. And he said that was no excuse, and told us about some famous actor who went on with a broken leg.'

'But I *didn't* feel well,' I said.

Thank goodness I hadn't allowed myself to cry for too long last night. I couldn't have faced Jimmy and all the cast with red, swollen eyes. My heart might be broken, but at least I looked, in my lovely costume, calm and beautiful.

'Iris!' Aly was whispering and nodding her lace-capped head.

I looked behind me. Jimmy was striding towards us. 'Iris,' he said, giving me, for a deadly moment, all his attention. 'No-one, and that includes you, walks out on my notes.'

'I'm sorry, Jimmy,' I said. 'I wasn't feeling well.'

'There's no room in the theatre for people with delicate health,' he said scornfully. 'Are you too frail to carry a packet of aspirin?'

I felt myself going hot under my heavy make-up.

'Don't do it again. Ever.'

And then, before I could reply, he had swept on to the props girl, who had put a chair six inches out of place.

I tried to breathe deeply in my tightly laced dress. At least I was angry again. That was better than moping. I swept onstage, ready to give the performance of my life.

And that was when Jimmy lost his temper and told me to stop acting and just sing.

I was raging inside, trapped in my ridiculous costume, when I wanted to scream and stamp with fury. But I folded my hands and sang my first solo and, later, my second, without a hint of emotion.

Jimmy wasn't going to have the chance to criticize my acting ever again.

After we'd rehearsed the curtain calls – in the hope that we'd actually *have* curtain calls – we all trooped offstage, everyone except me chattering and complaining.

'I was *so* nervous! Did you hear my voice shaking?'

'And Adrian missed his cue! I didn't know when to come in.'

'They lit my scene with Queen Victoria all wrong – there should've been a spot!'

The chorus of hysterical moaning and giggling swept past me. A year ago I would've been squealing about missed cues and lost props, but I couldn't bring myself to join in. I didn't care if my costume were too tight, or if Mrs Reece had taken my lullaby too slowly, I would just go through this show and get it over with, and then I'd never act again. I'd tell Mr Stoller that I wanted to train as a classical singer. I'd give concerts, appearing in a perfectly simple black dress (which would show off my red hair), and sing with such purity of style that leading critics would—

'Iris.'

Jimmy had touched my elbow. He had actually touched me! I shook myself awake. This was Jimmy beside me, yes, but Jimmy the bad-tempered, married teacher, come to tell me one more time that I was rubbish.

'What am I to do with you?'

Take me in your arms, kiss off all my make-up, I said to myself – before cringing with embarrassment. What if Jimmy somehow guessed what I was thinking? I made my face blank and concentrated on what he was saying.

'You've got a lot of talent. You sing beautifully for a schoolgirl. You've got stage presence. But you can't take direction! Either your performance is totally over the top, or, like tonight, you give nothing.'

'You told me not to act,' I said coldly.

'I didn't say stop living! A dead cat would've contributed more than you did.'

I felt as though Jimmy had shot an arrow straight through my heart.

I wouldn't cry. 'I doubt if a *dead* cat could reach top C,' I snapped back.

Jimmy began to laugh. 'Oh, Iris, I love you! If you were hopeless, I wouldn't keep on at you, but once or twice at rehearsals you were beginning to get it right. And that's what's so frustrating. I know you can do it, but I don't know how to help you. I'm as angry with myself as I am with you. If I can't get an intelligent, sensitive girl like you to act, I must be a useless teacher.'

I could hardly believe what I was hearing. For the first time since I'd known him, Jimmy was admitting that he might be wrong! It ought to have pleased me, but somehow I couldn't bear it.

'Oh, please, Jimmy, don't say that,' I said earnestly. 'You're a wonderful teacher. It's my fault. I'm a terrible actress, I'll never be any good.'

And I began to cry. Enormous hot round tears poured down my rouged cheeks.

'Oh, Iris, come here.'

Jimmy put his arms round me and gave me a hug.

As I leant against him, sobbing into his black T-shirt, I had the sensation that never before in my life had I been warm and safe and cared for and comforted. So this was what it felt like – and it was only going to last for a moment.

Sure enough, far too soon, he released me. 'Don't cry on the genuine antique.' He rearranged the lace shawl round my shoulders, and then dug into his pocket and gave me some paper hankies. 'No more advice. Just do what feels right tomorrow, but do it quietly, OK?'

'OK, Jimmy,' I said. I sniffed and dried my face (oh rats, just like feeble Janine) and turned away towards the dressing room.

Behind me I could hear him shouting: 'So what happened to Queen Victoria's spotlight?'

He had given me three hankies. Two of them were now damp, mascara-stained balls, but the third, which I hadn't used, I folded up into a very small square and tucked into my bra. When I got home I'd put it in the box where I kept Jean-Paul's iris-coloured scarf.

Chapter Ten

The atmosphere in the girls' dressing room was totally frantic. Everyone was nervous, and there was a lot of squealing and shrieking as people pushed around the mirrors, pinning up their hair or re-doing lipstick and eye-liner.

I sat quietly in my corner and looked around the room. One other person hadn't been caught up in the first-night frenzy. Janine. Like me, she was sitting apart, quietly absorbed in tying back her ringlets with a pink velvet ribbon. Despite her make-up she looked dreadfully white, and not at all like the carefree little girl whom she was playing.

For the first time I felt a real rush of sympathy, not just for Janine, but for her mother. I remembered the awful improvisation when I'd had to pretend to be dying. Was that how Janine's mother felt right now? Wondering if she were going to die. Wondering if she'd ever see Janine again.

That must be what Effie was feeling! Suddenly I saw her as a real person, and not as a made-up character. I *knew* what she was going through; I wasn't pretending, as I had during all those dreadful rehearsals. I could feel the terror which lay behind her apparent lightheartedness, a terror which never left her, day or night.

I remembered what Jimmy had said on the day of the improvisation: 'Use the feeling.'

I got up and left the noisy room, holding on tightly to the fear, not my fear of forgetting my lines or coming in late, but Effie's fear.

'Do what feels right, but do it quietly.'

I stood in the corridor, folding my hands around my embroidered purse. I was a proper, well-brought-up, Victorian young lady. My despair would remain concealed – almost.

'Beginners please!'

Now we were moving down the staircase, everyone suddenly silent except for last-minute whispers of encouragement.

Dinah, Aly, Morven and I stood in the wings, forced apart by the width of our crinolines. As we watched the stage the curtains swept back, and a group of girls wearing the traditional shawls and striped petticoats of Scottish fish-wives ran onstage, singing, to offer their baskets of herring to the Edinburgh housewives. More and more people crowded after them, businessmen, urchins, a nanny with two neatly dressed little girls, and more street sellers.

I seemed to be watching them all from terribly far away, as Effie must have done, wondering if she'd ever again be part of a happy, unconcerned crowd.

Then the opening number was over, the chorus left the stage, our chairs and sofa were arranged, and we four ladies took our places.

The lights went up and my companions began to gossip over their tea-cups. Aly and Morven, the visitors, have heard a rumour that Dr Simpson is performing ungodly experiments with a substance which will reduce the pain of labour. Is this true? Mrs Simpson, well-meaning but confused, doesn't know how to reply. The ladies declare that nothing could make childbirth less alarming, and Effie grows more and more frightened. Eventually, as the lights dim over the women on the sofa, I step into my spotlight and sing.

As I sang, I let Janine's mother's loneliness and fear fill my body, but I restrained the fear with Effie's strict code of manners.

When the song was over I sat down, realizing that I had finally stopped shaking.

Then scene followed scene until it was time for my second number. Now I'm lying on the sofa, wearing a white, lace-trimmed dressing gown. My baby is in a cradle by my side. Randal, playing my husband, and the nurse have just left, forbidding me to get up, but once they are safely out of the way, I cautiously rise to my feet. Then, picking up the baby, I begin to waltz around the room. As I dance, my long pale skirts swirl out under the lights, and with every step I feel happiness and freedom returning to me.

At last I sink down onto the sofa and, rocking the child, I sing Blake's Scottish lullaby.

It had been Jimmy's plan that the show should run on quickly and smoothly, without applause after each individual number, but as my last notes died away there was such a burst of clapping that Randal had to hold his entrance. For a moment, as the delight in being applauded rushed through me, I almost lost my hold on Effie's feelings. But I couldn't let go now! I mustn't be Iris, but a young mother, a little guilty at her stern husband's approach, but too happy to be really concerned.

As Randal entered I was safely back in character.

The show crept on. I appeared in some scenes, sat out others, sang in the chorus, and all the time I had a confused but powerful feeling that this time it was all *different*. My acting seemed suddenly to be in touch with an unexpected, deeper part of myself. Was this what Jimmy had been talking about all along?

When the curtain calls were over and we were all bouncing about the stage, high on excitement and applause, I looked across at him. He was trying to shoo us off the set.

'Yes, kids, you were all brilliant, but let's be professional here. The stage crew have to set up for tomorrow.'

Then he caught my glance, smiled, and gave me a tiny nod. I did a ridiculous, Victorian thing. I found that I'd clasped my hands against my heart. I remembered a poem we'd done once in English class: 'My heart is like a singing bird.' I'd thought it romantic rubbish but that *was* how I felt; as though my heart were singing. Jimmy thought I'd got it right! Perhaps I was an actress after all.

'You were different tonight,' said Rachel. She was taking off her make-up, and I caught her puzzled expression in the mirror. 'I don't know how exactly, just different.'

I looked around automatically for Aly, but she was in a corner with Janine. Janine was rubbing her face with cotton wool, while Aly unhooked the back of her dress. As I watched, Janine pulled on her jeans and jersey, grabbed her bag and, without bothering to undo her ringlets, pushed her way through the other girls to the door. As she opened it I thought I caught a glimpse of Randal, waiting outside in the corridor. I must've been right because there was a chorus of indignant cries – 'Randal! What did you hope to see then?' – before the door slammed shut.

Aly, who was picking up Janine's stuff, turned

and saw me staring. 'Janine was in a hurry because, if she wasn't too late, she could phone the hospital and leave a message for her mum about how the show had gone.'

I shrugged and said nothing. I decided not to mention Randal. After all, he'd never exactly been my boyfriend. So what did I care if he preferred Janine's company to mine? At least I'd be safe from his teasing. And nothing really mattered besides pleasing Jimmy. And I *had* pleased him tonight. I'd somehow found the way of making my acting work.

I turned away from Aly, hardly caring what she was saying.

'Iris, you were wonderful!' Dinah rushed up and hugged me. 'I got shivers up and down my spine when you sang tonight.'

'But so were you,' I responded. 'That bit when you're begging Adrian to stop experimenting was so funny.'

The usual backstage giggles, compliments and moans were building into a crescendo, despite all the efforts of our dressers, Morven's mother and Mrs Reilly, one of the art teachers, to calm us down. But at last we all got ourselves into our own clothes, and then downstairs to where our parents and friends were waiting.

My family were spacing out their visits to the show. Maggie and Auntie Wyn had come tonight, and Gran was coming from Norfolk for the last night. Like her daughters, she can't sing a note, but she loves to hear me.

Coming down the stairs, I saw Maggie waiting with the other parents and I suddenly felt my old childish admiration for her. She looked so elegant! A lot of my friends' mothers are either the silk-scarf-

and-green-waterproof-jacket type, like Morven's mum, or the jeans-and-long-woolly-jumper sort, like Aly's. But Maggie was wearing the most beautiful grey silk suit, her usual high heels, and diamond ear-rings. Even though she is small and sturdy, she looked like some exotic animal who happened to be strolling through a farmyard of ordinary, domestic creatures.

I raced down to meet her. 'What did you think of the show? Did you enjoy it?'

'You were terrific, darling,' she cried, wafting Cinnabar towards me.

'Iris, your voice gets better and better.' This was Wyn, still wearing the shawl but, fortunately, no hat. She smelt of Amarige. 'I'll tell Gerry and Lou what they missed. They couldn't be dragged from their books.'

They both kissed me, and as we went out to Wyn's car I asked them which bits of the show they'd enjoyed most.

'Well, your songs, obviously,' said Maggie, 'but really, I enjoyed it all.'

'I expected it to be a bit boring; I mean, such a serious subject,' said Wyn, 'but it was very well put together. Your director must be brilliant.'

I glowed as though I had been praised myself. 'Yes, Jimmy's very good,' I said, trying to conceal my enthusiasm.

'I thought you didn't like him,' said Maggie.

'Well, his technique's totally different from Miss Kerr's,' I said. 'But I think we've all got accustomed to him by now.'

'It was certainly most original,' continued Maggie. 'And I loved the comic touches. Your friend William was absolutely amazing as Queen Victoria – and that little girl who played the

Simpsons' daughter, she was simply wonderful, wasn't she, Wyn?'

We had, by now, reached the car and Wyn was unlocking the doors. She was going to drop us off before driving back to her home in Islington.

'Yes, I loved that scene where she confronts the angry clergyman,' said Wyn.

'And I never thought I'd see Randal in one of those collars!' laughed Maggie.

My mother had been so carried away by the success of the show that she hadn't mentioned work or university once!

I settled into the back of the car, and fastened the seat belt. 'Of course,' I said casually, 'now you've seen the show, you can understand how impossible it would be for me to drop out. When we go to Edinburgh.'

'But I didn't think that was definite.' Maggie was in the front with Wyn.

'Jimmy said we'd go if *Anaesthesia* was successful. And it is. Look how many curtain calls we got!'

'We'll just have to wait and see what happens.'

'If the others go, I simply have to go with them,' I said. 'I can't let the group down.'

'You have a point there, Iris,' said my aunt.

'Oh, do be quiet, Wyn,' snapped Maggie. 'As I said, we'll simply have to wait and see.'

I leant back in my seat. I was perfectly certain that Maggie couldn't stop me going now that she had seen how important my songs were to the show. And Auntie Wyn knew that as well as I did.

No matter what Maggie's reason was for trying to prevent me from going to Edinburgh, she wasn't going to succeed.

Chapter Eleven

Sure enough, when we came back to school after Christmas, the first thing we heard was that Mrs Jennings and Jimmy had agreed that we'd take *Anaesthesia* to the Fringe.

I was particularly excited because my Christmas had been a bit dismal and I needed something to look forward to. I'd gone to the usual parties, and Maggie and I had had our traditional non-cooking meal in a restaurant with some of her other single-mother friends, and I'd had some great presents, but the problem was – I missed Aly. Nothing was the same without her. Last-minute shopping, secrets, wrapping pressies . . .

One afternoon, early in the holidays, I'd gone round to her house with the idea that we should make Christmas biscuits together, something sweet and old-fashioned which we used to do when we were little kids. I'd even brought the ingredients with me, so when Aly's little brother, a computer freak who never talks to girls, opened the door and waved me upstairs, I dashed in and up, still carrying the poly bag.

Aly is a secret classical music fan, so something was fluting away in her room. I ran upstairs towards the melody and flung open the door. Aly and Janine were sitting on the floor, surrounded by boxes and bags and rolls of Christmas paper. As I stood there, they both looked up at me like little surprised woodland animals. I almost expected them to take fright and hide under the bed.

'Why, Iris,' said Aly. 'I never heard you come in.'

She was wrapping something in pink tissue paper while Janine held the sellotape and scissors. I thought for a moment that the present might be for me, and that was why they both looked so awkward, but Aly unfolded the paper to show me what was inside. 'Look, this is Janine's welcome-home-from-hospital present for her mum.'

It was a bedside lamp with a pink glass shade.

'Gorgeous,' I said. 'Stunning.'

'We won't be much longer,' continued Aly, 'and then I'll make some tea.'

'And we've got some lovely Christmas biscuits,' chimed in Janine. 'Mum and I always used to make them, but as she can't do it this year I made them with Aly instead. You twist them in circles so you can hang them from your tree with ribbon.'

'Oh yes, I know the sort. Yummy. I *love* Christmas biscuits.'

Aly bent over the lamp, tucking the paper around the corners. Then she looked up and met my eye, looking confused and unhappy. I knew exactly what she was thinking. She was remembering us both standing on chairs in order to reach the kitchen table while her mother helped us to plait the dough and wind it into rings.

'*Double* yummy,' I said. I put my carrier bag down in the corner, turning down the top so that the butter and sugar were hidden. Then I plumped myself down on Aly's printed Indian bedspread. 'I'll just watch until it's bikkie-time,' I said brightly.

Aly and Janine continued to wrap presents while I made jolly remarks about the things they had bought. Janine didn't say another word, and although Aly chattered back, I guessed that she felt guilty for sharing our childhood pastime with Janine. Every so often she gave me a pleading look, as though begging me to either forgive her or shut up.

But somehow, once I'd started being mean, I couldn't stop. I admired the neat way in which Aly tied bows. I admired Janine's hair, still soft and curly. And when we eventually went down to the kitchen, I went on and on about the wonderful biscuits.

'These are *delicious*,' I said, licking the buttery crumbs off my fingers. 'Do you remember, Aly, we used to make them when we were little? In this very kitchen.' I smiled gaily.

'Yes,' said Aly. 'Would anyone like some more tea?'

Janine shook her head and clutched her mug. She knew that something was going on, but didn't know what it was.

'Yes,' I continued. 'We used to have such merry, innocent fun.'

'Really?' Janine looked doubtful, as though that were the last sort of fun she would suspect me of having.

I looked back at her. Less mousy than she used to be, her brown eyes touched up with a little liner and mascara, but her chin still sharp and her nose still long – what was her attraction?

'I'll have to go now, Aly,' she said. 'Thanks so much for helping me, I'm just useless at wrapping things nicely.'

'Oh, I'm sure you're being too modest,' I said. 'Tell you what, I'll walk up the road with you. You've given me such a good idea. I'll make some of these biscuits for Mr Stoller. My singing teacher. He'd love them.'

Now Janine was looking as embarrassed as Aly. I got up and put on my jacket, a ridiculous fake fur which I'd got in the market.

'He's a wonderful teacher. If you ever want to expand your voice, Janine, he's the person to go to.'

'I'll just get my things.' Janine hurried out of the kitchen and ran upstairs.

'I'll help you.' Aly went after her.

I virtuously washed our mugs and plates and wiped the crumbs off the table. Then I picked up my bag and strolled into the hall, singing the chorus of 'Hark, the Herald Angels Sing'.

'Ah, Iris, I knew it must be you.' Aly's father popped out of his study. His bearded, bespectacled face wore a look of annoyance.

'Yes,' I said. 'It's me, the Christmas sunbeam, but don't worry, I'm going whenever Janine's ready.'

'Ah, yes, Janine,' he said absentmindedly, 'the quiet friend.' And he disappeared behind his door.

I thought of sparing Janine the agony of my company by going right then, but at that moment she and Aly came down, both wearing coats.

'There was too much for Janine to carry by herself,' said Aly.

'Fine,' I said. 'Let me take something.'

So we set off together, three jolly chums laden with Christmas gifts for a bedridden mother.

'Pity it's not snowing,' I said.

After that episode, I didn't see Aly alone again for the rest of the holidays, and when we did meet, in a crowd, we were both cool and polite. But I refused to be upset. I decided that I'd forget about trivial things like friendship and concentrate on my singing and acting. I'd make Jimmy proud of me. I knew he was never going to fall in love with me, but I'd make him look at me again the way he'd looked on the first night, with appreciation and respect. I didn't care how much hard work it took, I was going to do it!

It was lucky that I had this to think about because, the first day back at school, Aly wasn't waiting for me on the corner. I'd been pretending to myself that I wouldn't mind if she wasn't there, but when I came out of my gate and saw the empty street, it suddenly seemed impossible to keep on walking. I mean, the street wasn't really empty, there were little kids racing to school and business people getting into their cars, but it felt empty without Aly's familiar figure, hair fluffing out over her collar and her thin black woolly legs ending in ridiculously big boots.

I started to walk slowly towards school. I was being completely calm about this.

When I reached our classroom I saw Aly at once, chatting to Janine and Dinah. As I approached my desk she left the others and came to meet me. She was looking frightened but determined, a very characteristic Aly expression, which meant she was about to do something that was difficult but that she considered right.

'I'm sorry I didn't wait for you this morning,' she said, 'but I'm going to go round by Janine's from now on.'

'That's fine by me.' I began sorting out my books for the first lesson.

'It doesn't mean we have to stop being friends.'

'Rubbish,' I said, keeping my voice down. I

wasn't going to squabble in public. 'You've obviously decided who your real friend is. Don't let me stop you.'

'Iris.' She looked at me appealingly but I stared back, stony faced, determined to hurt her feelings as she was hurting mine.

'You might have some sympathy for Janine. You were just horrible to her that day you came round to my house.'

I wasn't going to be childish and declare that Aly and Janine had been horrible to me by making biscuits in secret.

'Sometimes I think you've got no feeling for anyone but yourself.' And Aly spun round and marched back to her friends.

No feeling! I remembered how I'd been flooded with sympathy for Janine's mother and how I'd used that feeling in my performance. Aly, who thought she knew me so well, didn't really know me at all. I was a much deeper and more sensitive person than she imagined.

'Iris, isn't it great news about Edinburgh?' Rachel had come up behind me, her usually serious face flushed and excited. 'You'll be coming, won't you?'

'We're definitely going?' I said, relieved to have something else to think about.

'Morven says so.' She gestured towards Morven, who was holding forth to a group of her followers. 'Apparently Mrs Jennings got in touch with her mother about fund-raising.'

Morven's mother, Mrs Normansby, does a lot of work on the Parent Teacher Association.

'But just because Morven says—' I began.

'No, there's going to be an announcement or a letter home or something.'

Rachel was right. As she spoke, Mrs Reece came in and began handing out the letters, which informed our parents that the school was sending a group of pupils to take part in this year's Edinburgh Fringe.

I was glad that the news came when it did, because everyone was too involved and excited to pay much attention to the fact that Aly was now Janine's best friend and not mine. Of course, it was too much to expect that no-one would notice, and I did catch a bit of smirking and giggling from Morven and her friends, but I held my head up and carried on as though nothing had happened.

However, I was very glad to leave school at the end of the day. I trudged off into the cold, not waiting to see if anyone else was coming in my direction.

'Where's Aly?' Randal had caught up with me. He was wearing a very old overcoat, several sizes too large for his bony frame.

'Are you playing at being Sherlock Holmes?' I said, pointing to the tattered checked tweed.

'Isn't it wonderful? It was my grandfather's. Perhaps it'll help me to track down Aly. Why isn't she trotting faithfully by your side as usual?'

'Oh, she and Janine are probably making a patchwork quilt together.'

'Not really? Why? Oh, I see, for the wonderful Garcia baby.'

'No, it was a joke,' I said coldly, quickening my pace so as to get rid of him all the sooner.

'I still don't see what you've got against Janine,' he said, easily keeping up with me. 'I got to know her quite well when we were doing the show, and she's really nice.'

'Well, of course you'd think that! She was being all sweet and little and brave because her mother was ill, and that's exactly the sort of stuff that guys fall for.'

'Well, Iris, even for you, that's a mean thing to say!'

Randal had actually been shocked out of drawling and spoke quite sharply. 'Janine was being brave. There was her mother in hospital, and she was carrying on with the show.'

'But she made sure everyone *knew* that she was carrying on bravely. I mean, all that crying because her mother couldn't see her act, and then rushing away early so's she could phone her.'

'She wasn't pretending to be upset. I gave her a lift home on the first night, so I know.'

So I'd been right! Randal *had* been waiting for Janine that night. This somehow made me angrier than ever. 'I didn't say she wasn't upset. I said she made sure everyone knew how *wonderful* she was being.'

'I think you must be just about the most unsympathetic person I've ever met.'

Randal was almost repeating Aly's words. All sorts of angry feelings began to surge about inside me. It wasn't true. I wasn't that horrible, cold-hearted person! 'I am so sympathetic! How could I *act* if I weren't sympathetic! That's how I acted the part of Effie. I was thinking how miserable and frightened Janine's mother must be, wondering if she were going to die, and I used that feeling to create my part!'

'You were pretending you were Janine's mother when you were acting?' Randal slowed down and faced me.

'Yes, more or less.'

It was really cold. I shivered and clutched the pile of books and ring-binders which I was carrying.

'I think that's sick,' said Randal.

'What do you mean?'

'I mean, that's taking something that belongs to someone else, and then just using it for yourself. And not just anything, their *feelings*.'

'But that's what acting's about,' I said. 'Jimmy says you have to use your real feelings to make your work truthful.'

'But *your* feelings, not stealing someone else's!'

'Oh, for heaven's sake, Randal,' I shouted at him, I'm only *sixteen*! I haven't had enough experience to play a part like Effie based on my own feelings, so I've got to use someone else's and *imagine* what they feel. If you can't see that, it explains why you're such a rotten actor. You wouldn't recognize a feeling if it jumped up and hit you in the face.'

The sight of Randal just standing there, silent, in his ridiculous coat, infuriated me. 'In fact, you're frightened of feelings, your own and other people's, and that's why you've always got to laugh and tease. You're scared to take anything seriously in case it hurts you. You're just an emotional coward!'

'Well,' said Randal, in a low, furious voice which I'd never heard before, 'perhaps I'd rather be an emotional coward than have so few feelings of my own that I have to pinch someone else's.'

And he swung round and marched away.

I discovered that I was literally jumping up and down on the kerb with fury. I'd never speak to Randal again. And how dare he say I had no feelings when I was absolutely *awash* with them! All my misery at losing Aly and loving Jimmy and having no father and Maggie trying to prevent me from going to Edinburgh was almost too much for me to bear, and here was Randal saying I had no feelings!

And then, as though all my separate problems had boiled up, in my anger, and run into one another, I suddenly saw something totally obvious. Perhaps there was a connection between the last two of these things: my unknown father, and Maggie's unwillingness to let me go to Edinburgh. *Perhaps my father was in Edinburgh*!

Now that I'd thought of it, I couldn't imagine why it hadn't occurred to me earlier. Although I'd been mostly taken in by Maggie's mutterings about work and exams, I'd still suspected that something else was worrying her – and this must be it. My lost father.

I realized that I was standing in lightly falling snow with my mouth open, like some sort of idiotic statue. I pulled myself together and continued walking, trying to look as though my world hadn't suddenly turned upside down.

The quarrel with Randal was forgotten. I had to get home so's I could phone Aly – but Aly would be with Janine! And after what had happened this morning, I felt that I could hardly tell her my suspicions. But she'd be sorry for shutting me out when we got to Edinburgh and I casually remarked that my father was coming to see the show.

'Your dad?' she'd say, overcome with amazement. 'But I thought you didn't know anything about him.'

'Just a little detective work,' I'd reply. 'It wasn't difficult once I had the first clue. And of course, he was dying to meet me . . .'

The daydream had carried me to my front door. I let myself in and went straight to the kitchen for some coffee.

Maybe he really *was* dying to meet me? I paced round the table with my mug, too excited to sit down. Was Maggie hiding me from him? It was an enticing idea, but I had to admit that if she wanted to hide a child she'd have changed her name or fled the country or at least arranged an unlisted phone number – none of which she'd done.

So perhaps he already had a family and he'd simply cast Maggie aside when she got pregnant? Yet it was hard to imagine casting aside someone as self-confident and independent as Maggie. She must've left him.

But I would soon find out because I had something which would force Maggie's hand – the school letter announcing the trip to Edinburgh. I laid it on the table, all ready to show her when she came in. One whiff of opposition and I'd confront her with my suspicions and demand to know the truth.

Chapter Twelve

However, when I gave Maggie the letter she simply glanced at it, said she'd talked the matter over with Auntie Wyn, and it would probably be quite a worthwhile experience for me to go!

'But I thought you were so worried about my work?' I said, scarcely able to believe my ears.

'Well, I was, but now that I've seen the show, I realize how important a member of the team you are. They'd never get anyone to play that part as well as you do.'

And Maggie actually smiled at me proudly and fondly, like she used to do when I brought home a dried pasta mosaic or a papier-mâché mouse.

'Oh well, thanks,' I said, sinking into the rocking chair.

I could scarcely be annoyed now that I'd succeeded in proving to Maggie that I was indispensable to the show, but I did feel a bit deflated. I'd been looking forward to a big dramatic scene in which Maggie would reveal the truth about my father, but here she was, calmly saying that she had no objection to my going to Scotland!

I decided that I must've got carried away in the aftermath of the scene with Randal and simply imagined the whole thing. It was lucky that I hadn't been able to tell Aly, or I would've looked a fool as well as feeling one.

'I think I'll just do some maths before supper,' I said, and I slunk off to my bedroom.

All in all, the spring term had got off to a terrible start, but I consoled myself with the thought of seeing Jimmy again and impressing him with the way in which I now brought genuine feeling to my work. However, no matter how hard I tried during the acting exercises which he set us, I never seemed to recapture that magic which had lit up my performance as Effie. And the worst of it was that Janine was becoming better and better. She really shone as an actress. The only thing that prevented me from giving up in despair was that Jimmy had actually stopped teasing me.

'You're trying too hard, Iris,' he said. 'It's an error on the right side, so I'm not telling you to stop working. Just let the part unfold rather than forcing the pace. Then you'll get somewhere.'

So I decided that if I couldn't dazzle Jimmy with my acting, I'd do it as a prize fund-raiser. As Randal had pointed out when Jimmy first raised the subject, performing on the Fringe was going to be very expensive. Besides the cost of renting a hall and accommodation, there would be transport and publicity to pay for, and we'd probably need to hire extra lighting equipment and rebuild some of the sets to fit a new stage. The parents of all the kids involved were going to contribute towards food and accommodation, and Mrs Jennings had agreed to make a donation from the school funds. Fortunately for us, various wealthy old Blacklockians had left legacies to the school in memory of their happy childhood days, and this money was available for cultural causes. And to raise the rest, Mrs Normansby and a committee of parents were organizing all the usual jumble sales, silent auctions and sponsorship events.

I had immediately had the idea of doing a singathon. I'd get people to promise an amount of money for each song I could sing in an evening. However, when I told Mr Stoller my great idea, he soon flattened me.

'No, Iris!' he cried in absolute horror. 'I can't think of a better way of ruining a young voice!'

'But it's to raise money for the show,' I said defensively.

'Sure, sure, but what's the point of raising money for a show you won't be able to sing in because by that time you'll be making a miserable noise like a corncrake?'

I didn't actually know what a corncrake was, which made the threat even more alarming.

'If you want to be a nightingale, Iris, you must relax, and allow your voice to soar, not belt out numbers like one of your rock singers.'

Everyone seemed to want me to be relaxed and unfolded, so on the way home from Mr Stoller's I bought a book on meditation and the most soothing poster I could find, a print of waterlilies on a dark-blue lake. From now on I'd meditate every day in front of the lilies until I became totally peaceful.

'Iris, what's happened to you? You're singing like an angel,' Mr Stoller would say, while my acting would move Jimmy to tears of delight.

'That was so beautiful, Iris. Now that you've found your true, calm centre your work has so much depth and profundity.'

'How do you do it? What's your secret?' This would be Janine, looking on enviously.

'Oh, it's nothing special,' I would say, bowing my

head with modest grace. 'When one finds oneself, then it's so much easier to unite artistry with technique.'

I fell over the kerb. Well, until all that happened, I'd work at being relaxed, or die in the attempt.

The weeks trailed by fairly miserably. The meditation didn't seem to be having much effect on either my singing, my acting, or my low spirits. I still wasn't speaking to Aly and Randal had stopped speaking to me. I'd had to give up my singathon and resign myself to helping at the jumble sale. And whenever I saw Jimmy, now all muffled against the cold in a big black overcoat, my heart still gave a silly thump before settling back to its usual dull ache.

Each drama class invariably started with some of the girls, led by Dinah, asking eagerly after the pregnant Tilda. I was determined not to join in these cosy sessions – and still less would I demean myself by taking part in the latest craze: making presents for the baby. The most unlikely people were working on tiny garments. Sarah, who can barely do a simple equation, somehow managed to make an incredibly complicated jacket, all lace and scallops.

'Oh, it's easy,' she said, the fashionable dark-purple wool which she had chosen flying through her fingers. 'My gran taught me to knit.'

Actually, my gran is also great at knitting, but it never occurred to me to ask her for lessons. I was going to stay at the farm for the Easter holidays, but I suspected that I'd left it too late for a crash course. Even if I wanted to give Jimmy's baby a present, which I didn't. Jimmy may have been nice to me once, out of pity, but I wasn't going to do anything soppy for him, like knit baby clothes. No way.

One Saturday afternoon at the end of February I found myself wandering dismally round Camden Market. I normally adore the market – in fact, I usually buy all my clothes there, to Maggie's disgust – but it wasn't the same, being by myself. It was a non-singing day, but I hadn't had the heart to fix anything up with Dinah or Rachel. Asking someone else to come out with me would just make it clear that Aly was no longer my friend.

When I eventually got cold and bored, I went into a café, bought a *cappuccino*, and settled down by the window. I was scooping up the delicious froth with my teaspoon when someone said: 'Iris? Is it OK if we join you?'

I looked up. A very pregnant young woman was standing beside the table, smiling at me. She waved towards the counter, where I saw Jimmy standing in the queue. 'I'm Tilda.'

'Oh, of course,' I said, hastily moving my bag and pulling out a chair for her. One moment I was lost in a dream, and the next I was speaking to the woman who ought to be my arch-enemy, Jimmy's wife.

Tilda sat down gratefully, sideways to the table. 'I used to love going round the stalls,' she said, 'but I'm the wrong shape now.'

She was almost as dark as Jimmy, but with pale, clear skin, and her fine black hair was cut in a neat bob. With her cloak and red muffler and bright brown eyes, she looked like a little girl on an old-fashioned Christmas card. To complete the pleasing impression she was unexpectedly making upon me, she said: 'Jimmy tells me you've got a lovely voice.'

'Really?' I said. 'He's usually telling me how useless I am.'

'Oh, but that's a compliment! He wouldn't bother unless he thought you had potential.'

'Really?' I said again. All my social skills seemed to have deserted me.

'Oh yes. I'm so sorry I wasn't able to see the show, but I was working.'

I realized that I ought to know what Tilda did, but if Jimmy had told us, I'd obviously blanked it out.

However, before I could look even stupider, she continued: 'I'm in stage lighting. It was my last job before I had to give up – I can hardly climb ladders in this condition!' And she patted the bulge under her jumper.

'Are you going to go back once the baby's born?' I asked politely.

'I'll give myself some time off, but then it'll depend on finding someone to look after the baby. The hours are so irregular in the theatre – but you'll know that.'

'I suppose it would be easier if you had a normal job.' Despite myself, I was being drawn into the kind of baby conversation which I'd been avoiding at school for weeks.

Tilda untied her cloak and pushed up the sleeves of her big cable-knit jumper. She had very small white hands which it was impossible to imagine rigging lights.

'It certainly would,' she said, 'but a normal job would be so boring. Don't you feel the same?'

'Oh yes! I've never wanted to do anything but go into the theatre, but my mother really disapproves.'

'I didn't know your mother felt like that.' Jimmy

had joined us with a black coffee for himself, and a glass of milk and a huge slice of chocolate gâteau for Tilda. 'Iris, can I get you anything else?'

'No, thanks, I'm fine,' I said, although I couldn't help looking wistfully at Tilda's plate. But it was bad enough being a friendless, hopeless actress without being fat as well.

'Here you are, baby,' said Tilda, digging her fork into the cake so that the cream squished out alluringly between the layers. 'I hope you like chocolate as much as I do. And don't worry about the vitamins; spinach for supper, I promise.'

Jimmy sat down. He was wearing his big black coat, which he now unbuttoned, and a felt hat of the type worn by gangsters in old movies.

He grinned at me, and I looked down into my coffee so that he wouldn't see the expression in my eyes.

'Your mother seemed quite enthusiastic about the show when I met her.'

'She thought the show was good, but she can sort of accept that because it's just school. What she doesn't want is for me to be *serious* about the theatre.' Both Jimmy and Tilda were now looking at me sympathetically. 'I mean, she was really against my doing the Fringe, but she seems to have come round to it.'

'You not do the Fringe!' Jimmy sounded gratifyingly dismayed. 'You're our star singer! Blake would have to take the lullaby down about an octave if anyone else were singing it, and then we'd lose that unearthly effect of the high notes.'

I felt as though I'd grown wings and were hovering somewhere just below the ceiling. Fortunately, the part of me that was still at the table tried to behave sensibly and modestly. 'But a lot of that's just technique,' I said. 'I've been having singing lessons for years.'

'Don't knock technique,' said Jimmy. 'That's one of the things I keep trying to drum into you kids. It doesn't matter how much emotional involvement you bring to a part if you don't have the technique to control it.'

'But that's just my problem! Either I'm too much involved or not enough. I never seem to get it right.'

'You got it right when it counted. You were good as Effie. Despite everything.' And he gave me a little, sideways grin.

I seemed to soar still higher, out of the café door and up into the cold spring sunshine. 'But I've never managed to do it *again*,' the sober part of me said.

'Give us both a break! How long have I been teaching you?'

'Five – six months.'

'Then we've only just started.'

'But is it worth my while going on?' It was the question I'd been longing to ask him.

'Well, as a person who likes to eat regularly, I'd never advise anyone to go into the theatre.'

Tilda was eating her cake in huge mouthfuls. 'Rubbish,' she said, through the crumbs. 'You know you think it's worth starving for.'

'Yes,' he said. 'I suppose I do. But, Iris, do you?'

The most important moment of my life, and I was sitting at a café table, wearing my silly fake fur, and probably with *cappuccino* froth all over my mouth.

'Yes,' I said solemnly, 'I do.'

'There you are,' said Tilda. 'She's one of us.'

'But is wanting to do it *enough*?'

Jimmy rearranged his hat at an even more dashing angle. 'Oh, Iris, I can't tell you. It's not just hard work and ambition and talent, but luck, and that's the one thing you can't depend on.' He saw that I was looking downcast because he added: 'But you *can* sing.'

'And that counts for a lot these days, now that musical theatre's so popular,' said Tilda. 'I do wish I'd heard you. But I'm coming to Edinburgh.'

'Are you really?'

If anyone had told me an hour ago that I'd be pleased to hear that Tilda was coming to Scotland, I'd have totally disbelieved them. But I couldn't help liking her. She was so sweet and good-tempered, and she didn't seem to be at all impressed by Jimmy's posing. In fact, as she answered me, she leant over and jammed his hat down over his ears.

'Yes, the baby and I are going to chaperone all you girls and boys.'

'That'll be terrific!' I said. 'I bet none of the other companies will have a baby with them.'

What was I saying? I was starting to babble like Dinah. I ought to leave while I was still behaving like a semi-reasonable person. I scrabbled under the table for my bag and then stood up.

'I really have to go now. It's been great meeting you, Tilda.'

'And you, Iris. But I'll see you in the summer, if not before.'

'Well, good luck with the baby.' Oh no, I was starting to enthuse again! 'Bye, Jimmy. Thank you.'

I squeezed my way between the crowded tables and then turned to look back. Jimmy and Tilda both waved.

Once I'd left the café, I looked back again. I could see them through the window, heads turned towards one another, holding hands.

I sighed with a curious mixture of emotions. I

was so thrilled by Jimmy's encouragement, and so excited to have met Tilda – and yet seeing them together made my heart ache with loneliness. Being with Jean-Paul had been romantic and exciting, but I'd always known that it wouldn't develop into a real relationship. But what if Aly and Randal were right? What if I really were such a self-centred, unsympathetic person that no-one would ever love me? Well, I'd just live for my art. I'd be known as a performer who gave everything to her work, never frittered away her energy on casual affairs – I walked straight into someone, and immediately recognized the rough tweed in which my nose was buried.

'Randal! What are you doing here?'

Randal looked at me haughtily. He was wearing the famous overcoat and clutching a parcel which was clumsily wrapped in newspaper. He turned away from me without speaking, and all at once I understood something, just as, on the first night, I'd understood how Janine's sick mother must feel. Now, seeing Randal withdraw, I knew I'd hurt him during our quarrel because I'd spoken the truth. Behind his lazy, confident manner, he was just a little boy who was frightened to express his feelings in case he burst into tears. And he'd never forgive me if he thought I'd found out his secret.

'Randal!' I cried. I ran after him and touched his sleeve. 'I'm sorry for what I said back then. I didn't mean it.'

He actually flushed slightly, but still didn't say anything. How dare he make this so difficult? I took a deep breath. 'I was just being nasty because I was angry.'

'Well, I was angry too.' He was silent again. Then he said, very quickly: 'I'm sorry as well, I shouldn't have said that, about your acting. I've been thinking about it, and you were right.'

The lofty Randal admitted I was right! And he'd been thinking about me . . .

'People our age haven't always had the sort of experiences you need for playing an adult part, so I suppose you have to – well, borrow them.'

I was so glad to have him speaking to me again that I refrained from making any sort of I-told-you-so comment. Instead I pointed to his parcel. 'What's that?'

'It's a birthday present for my mother. Do you think she'll like it?'

He pulled aside the newspaper and revealed a pretty little china teapot, patterned with pink and yellow roses. Randal's mother is an interior decorator, the sort who likes gathered blinds and floral curtains with tie-backs, so I knew straight away that she'd love it.

'It's perfect,' I said enthusiastically.

'She collects Victorian china.'

I felt very touched to think of Randal spending his time searching out a suitable present when he could've been sleeping, or whatever he does on a Saturday afternoon.

'I bet she'll be really pleased that you went to so much trouble,' I said.

'I certainly hope so,' he said, grinning. 'The way she feeds us, she doesn't really deserve a culinary gift.'

I smiled back. I hadn't let myself realize how much I'd missed him. 'Do you know who I just met?' I said.

He had rewrapped the teapot, and we began to walk slowly up Camden High Street, side by side.

'Jimmy and' – I paused dramatically – 'Tilda!'

'You met the mystery wife! Well, you'll be the envy of every girl in Blacklock's. Do you know, Iris, I think you must be the only female in the entire school who's been too sensible to either fall in love with Jimmy or become besotted with this wretched baby. Even Rachel keeps going on about it – and as for Janine and Aly, you can't see them for knitting wool!'

Randal had said something unkind about sweet little Janine! I smiled demurely. 'Oh, I think it's rather lovely. Janine and Aly are making a patchwork quilt together. They're knitting alternate squares and—'

'I thought you said it was a joke, when you said they were making a patchwork quilt together.'

'Well, it was a joke which came true,' I said, more sourly than I'd intended.

We walked on a bit further in silence.

'What happened with you and Aly?'

I think it must've been the first serious question which Randal had ever asked me. Anyway, it felt too serious for me to laugh, or evade the issue.

'She decided that she liked Janine better than me.'

'But couldn't you all have been friends?'

'Well, if Aly and I were together, Janine wouldn't join in. And when Aly and Janine were together, they sort of shut me out.'

I remembered the Christmas biscuits and had to blink hard. Fortunately I was wearing waterproof mascara.

'But you and Aly have been friends since primary!'

I nodded without speaking. I felt Randal looking at me, and then, without a word, he took my hand.

I was so surprised I could hardly keep walking in a straight line. When I'd recovered enough to speak, I repeated: 'She just likes Janine better.'

'I can't think why.'

'But I thought you liked her too.'

'Well, I do. I mean, Janine's quite sweet. But she hasn't got your – well – personality.'

It was so odd to have Randal both holding my hand and being nice to me that I felt completely disorientated. If Dinah had been there, she'd probably have explained that some kindly planet was transiting my chart. Or perhaps the meditation was working and I'd become a nicer person without noticing.

It didn't seem safe to speak, so I squeezed Randal's hand, and we kept walking towards Chalk Farm, both of us looking straight ahead.

Chapter Thirteen

I didn't really expect a passionate romance to blaze up between Randal and me, which was lucky because when we approached the danger zone of Chalk Farm, where we might possibly run into some of our friends, he dropped my hand, put both arms round his parcel, and began telling me funny stories about disastrous presents he'd given his parents in the past.

I sighed quietly. I'd enjoyed holding his hand, especially now that I understood him better, and realized that even touching me was, for Randal, quite a dangerous emotional statement. For all he knew, I might have burst into tears and flung myself embarrassingly into his arms. I remembered when Jimmy had hugged me after the dress rehearsal and how *consoled* I had felt, almost as though someone loved me. Of course, Jimmy didn't *love* me, but it had felt as though he appreciated me, and that made me seem like a real person for once.

I caught myself up. What did I mean 'real for once'? I was real just now, wasn't I, clumping up Chalk Farm Road in my boots?

Randal was still talking. 'So when Dad opened the parcel, it was obvious that he had absolutely no idea what it was, just that it was something I'd made, so he said it was so great he'd take it into the office and keep it there, and then all his colleagues could admire it. And I believed him! But I *was* only five.'

He had moved away from me slightly. Did I need to feel close to a man to be real to myself? Rachel, the feminist, would be horrified at the very thought. But I'd felt real when I was with Aly.

A cloud of crossness and gloom descended on me. If my feelings about myself were always going to depend on the good opinion of another person, I might be in for a pretty dismal life.

I felt Randal looking at me.

'Yeah,' I said quickly. 'That happened to me too. I did this huge, blotchy painting of a dinosaur for my mum, and I even put it in a perspex frame, so she had to hang it up.'

But Jimmy *had* said I was the star singer.

We had reached Randal's turning.

But how would it feel if there was no-one around to say I was a star?

'Are you going to William's party?'

'Yes.'

'Then I expect I'll see you there.'

And almost before I had time to realize it, Randal kissed me on the cheek and disappeared down the road.

By the time I reached home I was completely exhausted by emotion, and had to lie down quietly under my duvet.

Randal didn't try to kiss me a second time, and I wasn't sure whether or not I was sorry. On the one hand, my heart was dedicated to Jimmy and my art; but on the other – if Randal had kissed me again, I'd have had a chance to find out exactly how I felt. I mean, the kiss had been over so quickly that there had been no time for anything beyond a surge of pleasure and amazement. Now, with Jean-Paul I'd known exactly what was happening . . . but Jean-Paul was both older and *French*.

I decided, over the next couple of weeks, that Randal was rather embarrassed by his show of emotion. He teased me more than ever – yet he was always waiting for me after school, and we quickly got into the habit of going round to each other's houses for a snack.

One day, I even found myself telling him my suspicions about my unknown father.

We were drinking Earl Grey tea in Randal's kitchen, which is done up in a style similar to ours, but featuring lots of fussy details, such as the Victorian china collection, and incredibly frilly net curtains.

'But I saw in the end that I was just being silly,' I concluded, when I'd told him the whole story. 'I mean, even if he *were* in Edinburgh, I'd be so unlikely to meet him.'

Randal had listened to my recital without one flippant remark. Now he said, perfectly seriously: 'But not nearly as unlikely as if he were in a huge place like London. Edinburgh's tiny. Ros went there a couple of years ago, and she said the centre was so small you could easily walk everywhere.'

Ros is Randal's elder sister, an appallingly brainy girl who occasionally drops in from Oxford and then treats her old home as though it were some inferior planet.

'And besides that,' he continued, 'if you were in a show, he might come and see it by accident.' His grey eyes were gleaming with excitement.

'But I've just told you,' I said, 'Maggie's stopped objecting. So that proves that I'd just got carried away.'

Randal didn't want to give up. 'Perhaps she's realized that she can't prevent you from going, so she's pretending to be laid back about the whole thing, while inside she's a seething mass of emotions.'

I felt that this was probably a very good description of how Randal himself approached life, but I couldn't have said so without jeopardizing our new relationship.

'Mmm,' I said, 'anything's possible with my mum.'

'At least she doesn't make you use place mats on the kitchen table,' said Randal, stroking the heat-resistant mats, each decorated with a different floral motif, which he'd placed carefully beneath our cups.

'True,' I said, laughing. 'That's one thing to be thankful for.'

I was glad to change the subject. However, when I got up to go, he said: 'You could try testing your mother. You know, say things like, you've heard Edinburgh's very small. And remember – Jimmy said we'd be doing some street theatre to advertise the show. Tell her we're going to have a really high profile.'

Jimmy had mentioned that we'd be performing outside at a place called the Mound, where performers could do bits of their shows in order to entice an audience into coming to see the whole thing.

'Randal, you're being ridiculous,' I said sharply. 'Maggie's been in a really good mood with me since I got that A for my last English essay, so I'm not going to start pestering her about Edinburgh again.'

However, as I was starting to discover, every time I said I'd definitely do something – refrain from auditioning, be nice to Janine, never speak to Randal again – I always ended up doing the exact opposite.

A couple of days later Jimmy announced that he'd be holding extra singing auditions.

'Unbelievable though it may sound,' he said, 'there are those amongst you who'd rather go to *Disneyworld* – Disneyworld! – than take part in one of the world's biggest cultural bonanzas.'

He was looking mock-seriously at Mary and Irina, who were going to America in the summer with Irina's family. They were both in the chorus, but Mary was my understudy and Irina had a solo verse in the fishwives' opening number.

'But we're *not* going to Disneyworld,' said Irina patiently for about the tenth time. 'We're going to Colorado to see the Grand Canyon. My father's a geologist and—'

'A likely story, madam,' said Jimmy, doing a Groucho Marx impression. He was in a particularly good mood – perhaps because it was so nearly the end of term and he'd soon have a break from trying to turn a pack of schoolkids into a troupe of artistes.

'Anyway,' he said, 'I was going to get the casting settled by the beginning of next term so's we can do a bit of rehearsing. Not too much – we don't want to be stale by August – but we may have to re-block some of the ensembles for a different stage. So, does anyone who hasn't got a solo think they could tackle one?'

There was a silence while people nudged one another, and then one hand went up – Janine's! Everybody except Aly and I looked surprised. Janine could act, but she was hardly renowned as a songstress.

'OK then,' said Jimmy. If he, too, were surprised,

he concealed it by bounding to his feet. 'What are you going to sing? Let's hear you.'

'Now?' said Janine. She was clutching her hands together in her lap and looking very much as though she wished she'd kept quiet.

'Certainly now. A real pro can perform at the drop of a hat.'

'But – but – Mrs Reece isn't here to accompany.'

'Who needs Mrs Reece?'

Jimmy swept to the piano, flung himself down onto the stool, and began to play, swaying backwards and forwards like a berserk concert pianist. Those of us who knew anything about music moaned at the cascades of wrong notes – but he *was* wildly funny.

'Enough,' he said, calming down. 'Now, Janine, try a couple of verses of Effie's first number. Come on.'

Janine got up hesitantly and approached the piano. I watched her closely. Although she still looked nervous, she was breathing properly, from her diaphragm. Mr Stoller had obviously been making her work hard.

Jimmy played the introduction fairly competently, and Janine embarked upon my song. I held my breath – and then let it out in a sigh of relief. For a terrible moment I'd imagined that Mr Stoller might have magically transformed Janine into a diva in the same way that Jimmy had transformed her into an actress. But I'd nothing to fear; for while Janine was now singing much better, on a scale (ha ha) of one to ten, she was only at about five and a half. Of course, considering that she'd previously been an inaudible two, it was a mighty leap, but scarcely earth-shattering. She sang prettily, and in tune, but although we could now hear every note, her voice was still very thin and breathy in the upper register.

When she'd finished, all the people who hadn't known about her lessons looked even more amazed. Aly, grinning wildly, led a round of applause.

'Janine, you're a dark horse,' said Jimmy, swinging round to face her. 'Come clean, who's been teaching you, Carreras, Domingo, or Pavarotti?'

Janine looked confused and fiddled becomingly with her curls.

'No, seriously,' said Jimmy, 'you must've been having lessons. Who's your teacher?'

I caught Janine glancing timidly in my direction. She obviously didn't want me to know that she'd been sneaking lessons from my teacher, but she looked so trapped and embarrassed that I couldn't help feeling sorry for her.

'It must be Mr Stoller,' I said, smiling graciously. 'He's the only—' I almost said, 'the only one who could make so much difference', but I mumbled to a halt and changed it to: 'the only really good teacher around here.'

Janine nodded, staring at the floor.

'Well, Janine, I'm impressed,' said Jimmy. 'A for effort. Are you still having lessons?'

She nodded again.

'We'll see if we can find you a little bit to sing in the show – and tell you what, you can be Iris's understudy.'

It was all I could do to hold onto the gracious smile. Have Janine as my understudy! I'd take vitamins every day from now until the festival was safely over. I'd even swallow cod liver oil if it would keep me healthy. Whatever happened, I couldn't fall ill and have Janine play my wonderful part.

Janine, meanwhile, was being infuriatingly meek

and modest. 'But, Jimmy, what about Effie's lullaby? It's terribly high. I couldn't manage it.'

'Oh, I don't see Iris collapsing on us,' said Jimmy, beaming at me in a way which made me feel better, 'but if the worst came to the worst, Mrs Reece could take it down for you.'

'But what about my own part?'

'For heaven's sake, girl, you've got an understudy too, haven't you? If you play Iris's part, Melanie plays yours. Now stop making difficulties, we've got work to do. Who else wants to sing?'

Janine had no choice but to stop protesting and return to her place, where she was soon whispering to Aly in a flurried manner.

Serves you right, I thought to myself. Just see what happens if you really have to sing my lullaby.

At the end of the afternoon Randal and I strolled home together. It was too warm and springlike for the grandfatherly coat, so Randal had been forced to wear his blazer like everyone else. However, he had livened it up with a frayed white silk scarf of the kind supposedly worn by fighter pilots, which he wore looped round his neck.

'Janine might've thanked you for getting her out of that hole,' he said. 'I suppose she didn't want to let on that she'd been having lessons from your precious teacher in case you tore her limb for limb in a jealous frenzy.'

'He's hardly my private property,' I said, adding airily: 'Anyway, I knew she was having lessons.'

'What?'

'I saw her bag hanging up in Mr Stoller's hall ages ago.'

'Why didn't you tell anyone?'

I shrugged. It seemed so long ago that I could

scarcely remember why I'd kept quiet. 'Well, it wasn't my secret.'

Randal looked at me almost respectfully. 'Iris, you're revealing unsuspected depths of character here – keeping your least favourite person's secret, and then smiling sweetly when she's made your understudy. Come and have a cup of tea so's I can go on enjoying your saintly company.'

The prospect of being generous about Janine for another half-hour, even with Randal, was too appalling to consider. 'Sorry,' I said, 'I've got some stuff to print out and I'll have to do it now in case Maggie wants to use the printer in the evening.'

That was the sort of technological excuse which Randal understood, so he said goodbye and then stood waving on his corner until I'd reached mine.

Maggie, unusually, was home before me. She was in the sitting room, her feet up on the sofa, leafing through *Marie-Claire* and sipping gin and slimline tonic. As Maggie hardly ever drinks spirits, this meant that she was celebrating some minor triumph, such as persuading her company to use a better grade of button on this year's polyester sundress.

'What do you think's happened?' I said, advancing over the Persian rugs towards my mother's oasis of gin and glossy magazines. 'That wretched little Janine's been made my understudy!'

I sat down crosslegged opposite the sofa, in the unlikely hope that my meditation pose would make me feel calmer.

'Janine? Is she the little girl who played Jessie?'

'Yes, that's her. The one with the soppy ringlets,' I said disgustedly.

'I thought she was very good – but can she sing?'

'This is the infuriating part – she's been having lessons in secret from Mr Stoller!'

Maggie laid down her drink. 'That's hardly a crime.'

I waved my hands in exasperation. 'I know, I know, it was just the sneaky way she did it, not telling anyone, and then when Jimmy asks, Who wants to sing? she puts her hand up, all, you know, "please sir, me sir", because she knows she's going to knock us all out with her silvery tones.'

Maggie laughed. 'Very well, but can she sing?'

'Oh, kind of, not too bad really, but she hasn't got my range.'

'Well, not many people have, darling.' My mother was riffling through the pages of her magazine. Then she stopped at some apparently fascinating article, read a few lines, glanced at me sideways and said: 'Of course, if you've got a reasonable understudy, it wouldn't be the end of the world if you didn't go to Edinburgh.'

I couldn't believe what she was saying. 'What the hell do you mean? You said I could go, you said it was a good idea, I thought it was all settled!'

I jumped to my feet. Somehow I had to release all the anger and suspicion which suddenly threatened to choke me.

'Calm down, Iris, I wasn't saying you couldn't go, just that this opens up new possibilities—'

Maggie had laid down her magazine and was regarding me in a motherly, concerned fashion which I found simply unbearable.

'Something's going on here,' I said. I was shocked at how vindictive I sounded, but I wanted to say something to wound and upset her. 'You don't want me to go to Edinburgh because you're afraid I'll meet my father.'

Maggie went absolutely white. I had no idea that this was something which actually happened, but it did. She went white. A tiny, professional part of myself began taking note of every detail: So that's how you look when you've had a shock. I must remember. Your face loses all expression and your hands begin to shake. They really do.

Maggie reached for her drink, which slopped about wildly in her trembling hand. 'Iris, what a crazy idea! All this acting really is going to your head.' She gave a little, husky laugh.

'But it's true, isn't it?' I said flatly. I was almost horrified at what I'd done. Maggie was usually so confident and assured; I'd never before seen her out of control.

She looked up at me, and something she saw in my face made her turn away. 'You're right,' she said quietly. 'He is in Edinburgh.'

She finished her drink, found a tissue, and began to dab at her eyes clumsily, as though it were something which she didn't often do.

I collapsed into the nearest armchair, feeling that I'd won a terrible unnecessary victory. Neither of us spoke for a moment.

Then Maggie said: 'How did you find out?'

'I didn't. I guessed.'

'Wyn was right. She always said I should've told you more about your father.'

'More! You never told me anything!'

'But there wasn't much to tell! Your father was a lot younger than me. I met him when we were both working for Truelove Lingerie. He came for a few months to gain more marketing experience before being sent back to the Scottish branch. He was extremely good-looking and, I suppose, to him I seemed very – sophisticated. And so—'

Maggie hesitated.

'You had an affair?'

She nodded. 'He'd never lived in London before, so I showed him the best places to eat, things like that.' Maggie was trying hard to regain her composure. She raised her hands as though to illustrate her knowledge of the city. Then she let them drop into her lap.

'I didn't find out that I was pregnant until after he left.'

There was another silence while Maggie stared down at her hands.

'And did you tell him?'

'No. There wasn't any point. He'd gone home to get married.'

'He was *engaged* all this time you were carrying on? Did you know?'

This wasn't the way in which parents were supposed to behave.

Maggie looked at me almost pleadingly. 'Yes, he told me. It was – well – a last fling for him. He'd known his girlfriend for a long time—'

'A childhood sweetheart?' I said sarcastically.

'Yes, almost like that. They'd grown up together, and he said that once they were married he could never have hurt her by being unfaithful.'

'So there she was, up in Scotland, buying the bridal gown, and all the time he was sleeping with you!'

'Don't be so harsh, Iris! You don't know how these things happen!'

'So you never told him about me?'

'No. I didn't want to ruin his marriage. And I didn't need his money.' Even in the midst of her distress, Maggie looked proudly around our beautiful room.

'I'm surprised you went ahead and had me,' I said nastily. Somehow I couldn't get out the word 'abortion'.

'Oh but Iris!' cried Maggie, turning to face me, 'you don't understand – I wanted a baby so much! I was thirty-six when you were born, I thought perhaps it was too late.'

Then she seemed to realize she'd said too much, and she looked away.

I stared at her, clasping my cold hands together. 'Were you *trying* to have a baby?' I whispered.

Still looking away from me, she said: 'I told him I was on the Pill.'

I'd been leaning forward in my chair, but now I fell back against the cushions. So that was how Maggie saw me, as a child snatched, almost stolen triumphantly from fate! Now I could understand her attitude towards me. I had to succeed in everything I did in order to justify her action. She'd been determined that I would exist; and now I was paying the price by having to be perfect.

She was still talking. 'So when you told me you were going to Edinburgh I had these terrible fantasies that he'd somehow see you and recognize you and everything would come out and his family would be hurt—'

'But wait a moment.' I'd got my breath back. 'How do you know where he is?'

'The grapevine. He's still in the fashion business, although he's moved on from Truelove. I mean, I knew I was being paranoid about your meeting. Wyn told me I had to calm down, so I tried, but when you said you had a good understudy . . .' Her words trailed away, and she began to dab at her eyes again. 'I never meant to tell you like this.'

'Were you ever going to tell me at all?'

'Oh, when you were older. I imagined us having dinner together and my telling you in a civilized way. Not like this.' She looked helplessly around the room, as though the rugs and sofa and dark velvet curtains were somehow to blame.

I stood up. 'Is there a civilized way to tell your daughter she's a bastard who's been kept in the dark for years in order to protect a man she's never met? Haven't I got any rights here? Don't I even get to know his name?'

'But we don't need him, darling! Haven't we always been happy together, you and I?'

Like hell, I thought.

'Look,' I said. 'I don't want to upset him, or his precious wife, but I'd just like to know something about him. Is that so peculiar? I mean, do I look like him? Is he musical? Is it too much to ask if he's a nice guy?'

Maggie had finished wiping her eyes. Now, much more like her old self, she said: 'I'm not prepared to tell you anything about him until I can trust you not to go barging into his life and doing all sorts of harm. And if you insist on going to Edinburgh this year, I'm certainly not going to help you track him down. Possibly, when you're older, and can deal with this in a more mature way—'

'Older! Older!' I screamed. 'If growing older means I turn into a devious bitch like you, I hope I die young!'

And I ran out of the room, away from the echo of my words and Maggie's appalled face.

Chapter Fourteen

'Are you all right, Iris? You look awful.' Randal had been waiting for me on his corner.

I already knew how I looked, so this was the last thing I needed. Not only was my face pale grey, an even more unbecoming shade than white, but I somehow looked as I would when I was about forty, all creased and unfocused.

'Yes, I know I do,' I snapped back. I'd left the house without even seeing Maggie, so I'd no idea how she'd dealt with the crisis.

'Are you sure you should be going to school?'

I began walking and he fell into step beside me, actually slowing himself to my pace.

'We were right,' I said. 'My father is in Edinburgh.'

He stopped and looked at me. 'My God, Iris, what happened? How did you find out?'

I continued walking while I tried to sort out an edited version. 'I asked her, and she told me.'

'Does that mean you're going to get in touch with him?'

'No,' I said. 'Look, Randal, I'm sorry, I don't want to talk about it. Let's just leave it, OK?'

'OK.' He took my hand again, and actually held it all the way into school.

We met Aly and Janine on the front steps.

'Are you all right? You look terribly pale.' Aly

and I had only spoken in a constrained, polite sort of way for weeks, but now she sounded really concerned.

'Just a headache,' I said.

'Perhaps you should go home,' suggested Janine.

'I'm perfectly fine,' I said. How dare Janine tell me what to do?

However, by the end of the first class my head really did ache so badly, and I felt so miserable, that I sneaked out and went home without reporting to the school nurse.

Once there, I made myself a hot water bottle and lay under my duvet, hugging it until I fell into a feverish sleep.

When I woke up I actually *was* ill. My head throbbed and I was hot all over. I was quite impressed to discover that I was so sensitive that I could make myself ill with grief.

I got up, stumbled around until I found some aspirin, and then went back to bed. However, my room, which I've decorated like a Thirties' film-star's boudoir, seemed, for the first time, to be oppressive rather than glamorous, with its dark crimson curtains and leopardskin print walls. I lay there, watching the spots advance and retreat until Maggie came home.

Upon seeing me, she immediately went into a frenzy of maternal action, bringing me more aspirin and iced water and her unopened copy of the new *Vogue*.

Then she sat down on the end of my bed. I don't know which of us was the more embarrassed.

'I'm sorry about what happened yesterday,' she said. She was sitting sideways, with her hands folded in her lap and her legs neatly slanting. She looked like a rather nervous candidate being interviewed for an important job. 'I shouldn't have let you find out like that. I didn't mean it to be such a shock.'

'It's OK. I had to find out sometime.'

I was hating this. I really wanted her to go away. If this had been one of the American teenage soaps I sometimes watched on TV, we'd have been sobbing in one another's arms by now, all ready to start on a new, deeper, more meaningful relationship.

But I was *English* – no, even worse, half Scottish – and the last thing I wanted just now was a big emotional scene. 'And I'm sorry for what I said,' I added stiffly, pulling the duvet up to my chin.

Maggie looked relieved, and I suspected that she felt just as I did. 'That's all right, then, darling,' she said, getting up almost briskly. 'We won't talk about it again – and you won't mention it to Gran and Grandad, will you, when you go there next week? They don't know any of the details. They never asked.'

Typical of this screwed-up family, I thought. Secrets, mysteries, never asking, never telling. What chance did I have of growing up to be a normal person?

'Of course not,' I said.

Maggie bent down and kissed my cheek. 'I'll leave your door open. Call if you want anything.'

Oh yes, I thought, a real family, a father, someone to love me. One of these, please, or preferably all three.

I actually enjoyed my holiday in Norfolk in a bleak kind of way. Grandad's farm is very near the sea, so I spent hours and hours walking up and down the lonely beach, alternately brooding and declaiming some Shakespearean speeches which Jimmy had wanted us to learn. In between these gloomy pastimes I wondered what it would be like if Randal were with me.

When I'd done enough of all this, I'd come indoors and sit in front of the Aga and eat all the hot scones and pancakes and gingerbread which Gran had made for me. While I ate, I watched her knit.

Since seeing Tilda I'd somehow found myself going to a specialist wool shop and buying some lovely, soft, suitably non-sexually stereotyped lilac wool. However, when I examined Gran's huge library of knitting patterns, I realized that, as a novice knitter, I hadn't a hope of making even a dainty bootee. But Gran seized the wool as though it were buried treasure.

'Iris, girl, this is beautiful! I'd love to make it into a Shetland shawl for your friend. I haven't had any call to make one of those for years, and this would knit up like a dream.'

So I watched as, day by day, Gran's wrinkled old fingers transformed the wool into an enormous cobweb. The shawl was circular, with a scalloped edge and a lacy spiral pattern which spread outwards from the centre. When she had finished, Gran dampened her work, pinned it out on a board, stretching the edges tightly, and put it outside to dry. Then, when she removed the pins, the shawl was flat, and formed a perfect circle.

'Gran, that's magic!'

'Nothing to it,' she said, but I could tell that she was pleased to have impressed her cool grandchild.

Maggie came to pick me up at the end of the holidays, and we drove back fairly amicably. Since the big fight we'd both been making an effort to get along together. She'd stopped nagging about exams, and I was trying not to be an aggressive and sulky teenager. It was hard work, but at least we were speaking to one another.

The phone began ringing almost the moment we got home. It was Dinah. 'Where have you been? I've left dozens of messages on your machine.'

'I've only just got in. I was away being a granddaughter.'

'Well, listen to this: Jimmy's baby's a little girl!'

'When was she born? How did you find out?'

'The first week of the holidays. That makes her an Aries. She's got a very lucky chart.'

'But how do you know?'

'Because I worked it out, of course.'

'No, no, how do you know it's a girl?'

'I made Jimmy promise to call me the moment the baby was born so's I could get working on the chart. They're calling her Dorinda.'

'What an amazing name!'

'Isn't it glamorous? Dorinda Grace Garcia. What are you giving her?'

And before I knew where I was, I was launched on a girlie conversation about Gran's shawl and how nice it was to give handmade presents and wouldn't little Dorinda be fortunate if she inherited Jimmy's good looks.

'But Tilda's pretty,' I said. 'Not striking, like Jimmy, but very pretty.'

'I forgot you'd met her. Still, we'll all see her and Dorinda when we go to the Fringe. Just think – only three months and we'll be doing the show again. I can hardly wait!'

Once I'd rung off I went through to the kitchen, where Maggie was making us both *cappuccinos*.

'What do you think – Tilda's baby's a little girl!'

I could see Maggie concentrating. 'Tilda? Now she's—?'

'Jimmy's wife. Jimmy the drama teacher. They're calling her Dorinda.'

I realized that Maggie was looking a little puzzled by my enthusiasm, which was hardly surprising as I'd never before been excited about a baby. I made myself calm down. 'I just mean, it's so nice to have an unusual name. Like Iris. When Dorinda and I are both on the stage, at least our *names* will be unforgettable.'

Maggie laughed and handed me my coffee without the usual remarks on the uncertainty of a theatrical career. 'Was that Dinah on the phone? You had some other calls. William says to tell you he's having a party tomorrow, Rachel wants you to go on a demo, she didn't say against what, and Randal says he's back from Paris.'

Randal had been sent on an intensive French course to polish up his spoken language.

'Poor Randal,' I said. 'He was dreading that course. I'll go round after I've had something to eat, and test him.'

Randal opened the door wearing jeans and an unmistakably French linen shirt. He said: '*Enchanté, chère mademoiselle,*' and kissed my hand.

'Overwhelming,' I said. 'If you got that far in three weeks, what would've happened in six?'

'Come upstairs. The kitchen's full of intellectuals.'

'Ros is home?'

'Yeah. Anyway, *ma petite, j'ai un petit quelque chose pour toi.*'

'Really?'

'*Naturellement!* Do you mean you didn't bring me a pressie from lovely Norfolk?'

'If you'd seen the presents on offer in lovely Norfolk, you'd be thankful I didn't bring one. Your mum would've liked them though.'

Randal ushered me into his room. By sheer force of character he'd kept his mother's beloved frills at bay, and his room was therefore exactly like any other guy's, except that a lot of his books were by authors other than Stephen King and Terry Pratchett.

His current volume was lying on the bed, so I sat down to examine it. 'Who's Ernest Hemingway?'

'Incredibly famous American writer.'

'Oh. Right.'

'I forgive your ignorance. Now close your eyes.'

He put something small and square, but bulkily wrapped, into my hands.

'Now open.'

I was holding a folded duty-free bag.

'Now look inside.'

Next moment he was covering his ears as I began to scream: 'Oscar de la Renta! Randal, how did you *know*? That's my total favourite! I had the cologne once, but this is the actual *perfume*! Oh Randal!'

'I'd no idea you'd be so pleased. It's quite alarming. If a tiny bottle of perfume sends you into hysterics, I'd be terrified to give you anything bigger – a diamond bracelet, say.' He was grinning in a self-satisfied, masculine way.

'But how did you know?' I repeated. 'You must be psychic.'

'Nah. You and Aly were rabbiting on about perfume one day. She said her mum didn't approve of it, and you went into a rhapsody about this stuff.'

'But fancy you remembering.' I was really

touched, especially as the conversation must've taken place before Christmas. 'Thank you. It was sweet of you. I just can't say how pleased I am.'

'Go on then, take it for a test drive.'

He came and sat beside me.

I kicked off my sandals and sat crosslegged on the bed. Then I carefully unpicked the cellophane, opened the box, unstoppered the bottle, and dabbed some perfume on my wrist. 'Smell.'

He sniffed my wrist. 'Gorgeous.' He kissed the spot, then licked it. 'Tasty, too. Spicy. Warm undertones. Mmmm.'

I closed the bottle and put it carefully on the bedside table, along with Ernest Hemingway.

Randal pushed up my sleeve and went on kissing up my arm. I raised my hand and touched his silly, floppy, blond hair.

'Do you know, Iris,' he said, raising his head, 'I really missed you. I thought about you all the time.'

I let my hand slide down to the nape of his neck. 'What about the girls on your course?'

'Two sultry Iranian sisters, three awesome blondes, an incredibly buxom brunette, and I still thought about you.' He slid his hands round my back.

'I thought about you, too,' I said.

'Didn't Norfolk offer any competition?' he said, pulling me closer.

'No competition. I had no choice but to think of you.'

'All the time?'

'All the time.'

'Then you must've had a wonderful holiday.'

'Yes,' I said, 'but not as good as I'm having now.'

Then he kissed me properly and, after a moment, I shifted my balance so that I fell backwards onto the bed, taking him with me. However, when he raised himself on one elbow and began unbuttoning my shirt with his free hand, I said: 'Wait.'

'Too late.'

'No, does your door lock?'

'Didn't you notice? I locked it behind you when you came in.'

'So there's no escape?'

'Absolutely none.'

'Oh good.'

Chapter Fifteen

On the day of Jimmy's first class of the summer term at least half the girls turned up with parcels daintily wrapped in pink paper. Rachel, meanwhile, had organized the 'non-craftspeople', as she called them, into contributing money with which she'd bought gift vouchers from a babywear shop.

While we waited for Jimmy to appear, she and William argued about the wording on the accompanying card.

' "Non-craftspeople" makes us sound clumsy,' he said, making a show of being serious.

Rachel, taken in for once, drew up her arched black eyebrows. 'Do you really think so?'

'Yes. As a contributor, I'd prefer "intellectually able".'

'*William*. I can't say that, it makes the craftspeople sound intellectually challenged.'

'OK, then how about calling us "craftily challenged"?'

Rachel realized that he'd tricked her into a debate. 'I'm not discussing this a minute longer. I'm just going to get everyone to sign the card.'

'It's too small,' said William triumphantly.

Randal, who was sitting on the floor next to me, discreetly running his hand up and down my spine, said: 'Why don't you say "from all of us who felt unable to put our energy into the noble tradition of craftwork"?'

'Excellent!' said Rachel. 'William, you can't possibly quarrel with that, can you?'

'I wouldn't dare,' said William.

He and Randal winked at one another. They were still clowning behind Rachel's back when Jimmy walked in. He was wearing a Mafia-inspired outfit of dark trousers and waistcoat, white shirt, and his gangster hat, presumably to indicate that he was now Head of a Family. When he saw the pyramid of pink gifts, however, he stopped in mid-saunter.

'My God, what's this?'

'Surprise!' cried Sarah and her fellow craftspeople.

Jimmy staggered back dramatically. 'I'm only thankful I don't have to go through this on my own.'

He opened the door wider and Tilda came in, now perfectly thin in jeans and T-shirt, carrying a baby basket.

All the girls went 'Awww!' and rushed forward like one of the waves on my beach. I was swept along with them. I didn't care how uncool I looked, I was desperate to see Jimmy and Tilda's baby.

We crowded round the basket.

'She's perfect!'

'She's beautiful!'

'Look at her eyelashes!'

All the usual soppy comments were completely true. Dorinda's skin was the exact rose-white of the waterlilies on my poster, her hair was fine and soft and black like Tilda's, and she had an idiotically small version of Jimmy's elegant nose.

The boys, who had been exchanging cynical looks in the background, lounged forward to join us.

'I say, I say, I say, how can you tell that baby's going to be a star?' said William.

'I don't know, how can you tell that baby's going to be a star?' answered Randal.

'It's so obvious it's "star-ing" you in the face.'

Rachel turned her back on their antics and spoke up in her usual impressive manner. 'Jimmy and Tilda, this is from all of us who were unable to make presents,' and she handed Tilda the envelope containing the vouchers.

'That's so sweet of you, I don't know what to say except "thank you",' said Tilda, who was blushing with surprise and pleasure. 'I'd no idea we were getting presents.'

'Neither did I,' said Jimmy. He had sunk to the floor, and was fanning himself with his hat. 'This was just a little social visit because you'd all shown such enthusiasm over our offspring. We weren't expecting to rake in worldly goods—' and he waved his hat, actually overwhelmed into silence.

'In that case, you can give back the babywear vouchers,' said William irrepressibly. 'Who can tell when one of us will need them?'

'Shut up, William,' said Dinah. 'Dorinda Grace Garcia, here's your personal horoscope,' and she laid the elaborate chart on the baby's quilt.

Tilda then sat down beside Jimmy and opened all our presents, making suitably delighted noises. When she came to Gran's shawl, she cried: 'I was dying for one of these! I didn't think there was anyone left who could make them. Who knitted it?'

'My gran made it,' I said. At least I had one relative I could be proud of.

'I'm going to write to her,' said Tilda. 'Now, what will I open next?'

While Tilda continued unwrapping the presents,

I saw Jimmy take out his handkerchief and wipe his eyes in a very open, unBritish way. Perhaps he actually was Spanish?

As I watched him I tested my feelings. Did I still love him? Somehow, ever since I'd met Tilda, it was as though my love had expanded to include her, thus making it impossible to feel romantic about Jimmy. Yet I couldn't deny that I had a special feeling for him because he'd been kind to me, and because I felt that we were the same sort of people. And Randal? He was standing at the back of the circle, grinning, forgetting that he was meant to be bored. He caught my eye and moved round to stand behind me. I leant back against his long legs. Yes, I loved him, but our relationship still seemed so fragile and uncertain. I sensed that if he knew how well I understood the depth of his feelings, he'd withdraw, afraid of having his hidden emotions revealed. But Jimmy didn't conceal his feelings. He wasn't afraid of losing his temper, or showing affection, or even crying. The difference, I supposed, was that Jimmy, despite his constant showing off, was actually a grown-up.

I'd been staring at Jimmy in a daze while I had these deep thoughts. Now he grinned at me as he stuffed his handkerchief back in his pocket.

'Come on, people, we've got a show to put on! Tilda, get this infant out of here, there's no room for passengers on this trip.'

'But I can't carry all these myself!' protested Tilda, who was refolding all the little pressies into their wrappers.

'Carry the baby and put the presents in the basket,' I suggested.

'Iris,' said Jimmy, 'I'd never have suspected you of lateral thinking.'

Tilda lifted Dorinda out of the basket, and Dinah and I piled in the presents.

'Iris, you can take the loot down to the car. You're the person least likely to listen to a word I say, so it won't matter if you miss five minutes of my scintillating lesson.' He kissed Tilda and stroked Dorinda's face. ''Bye, love, 'bye, sweetheart. Randal, you escort them. Make sure this woman and child leave the building and don't let them back in.'

Randal said: 'Yes, sir,' and opened the door for us. Then we led Tilda down the corridor, Randal and I carrying the basket between us.

'I still don't believe it,' she said. 'I'd no idea Jimmy was so popular. He told me you all adored him, but I thought he was boasting as usual. Still, I'll see him in action as a teacher when I come to Edinburgh. Are you still coming, Iris?'

I found myself longing to tell Tilda what had happened. She was looking at me as though she were really interested in my answer.

'Yes,' I said. 'Well, there is a problem, but it's not going to stop me.'

I glanced at Randal. He was looking at me with the same expression as Tilda, and I remembered how I'd refused to talk to him about my father the day after I'd found out the truth. But somehow, with Tilda there, it didn't seem so difficult to speak.

'I've just found out that my father's in Edinburgh. That's why my mother didn't want me to go. They split up, well, before I was born, and now he's married and got another family, I suppose.'

They both stopped and stared at me. Tilda said: 'You've only just found out? You must feel awful about it!'

I shrugged and walked on, forcing Randal to

start moving with me. 'There's not much I can do about it.'

We went out through the main door and across the courtyard towards the Garcia vehicle, an ancient Citroën 2CV.

'Are you going to see him?' said Tilda.

'No.'

Tilda shifted Dorinda onto one arm, felt in her pocket and handed Randal the car keys. 'Open the back door, would you?'

Randal unlocked the door and we unpacked the gifts into the car. Then Randal leant over and put the basket in the back seat while I opened the side door.

'Does your mum not want you to see him?' said Tilda.

'Mmm. Well, he doesn't actually know that I exist.'

Tilda and Randal stared at me all over again.

'When Maggie found out she was pregnant they'd already split up, so she didn't tell him. Anyway, I think she sort of wanted to bring me up on her own. You know, as a feminist statement.'

I knew that I was waffling, but I somehow couldn't bear to tell them that my father had been engaged to someone else, and that my mother had been secretly determined to get pregnant.

'Well, I suppose I can understand that,' said Tilda, looking lovingly down at Dorinda, 'but it can't have been easy for her. I don't know how I'd manage without Jimmy, infuriating though he is.'

'But couldn't she tell him about you now?' said Randal.

'She said it would upset him. And his wife.'

'But isn't it upsetting you?'

'Well, it did,' I said bleakly, 'but I've just got to live with it.'

Randal came and put his arm round me, and we watched as Tilda returned Dorinda to her basket and fastened the safety straps. Then she shut the door and came to join us.

'I am sorry, Iris,' she said, touching my shoulder. 'This must be so hard for you. Tell you what, why don't you come and visit me after school some day? You'd be doing me a favour; I get so bored being at home when I'm used to working. I'll give you the address and phone number.' She took a notebook out of her bag, scribbled on a page, tore it out, and handed it to me.

'Really? I'd love to.' I put the address in my pocket, feeling ridiculously cheered up.

'Of course. Now I'll have to go before her royal highness wakes up. 'Bye, Iris, 'bye, Randal,' and she kissed us both in a theatrical way which reminded me of Jimmy.

We stood on the kerb and waved as she disappeared.

'I wish you'd told me all that before.' Randal turned back towards the main entrance and I fell into step beside him.

'I'm sorry.'

'I did feel a bit hurt when you wouldn't talk about your father, but I thought I probably deserved it. After all, I'm always laughing at you. It's not surprising if you don't trust me.'

'Oh no, Randal! It's not like that!' I cried, putting my arms round him. I couldn't bear to think I'd upset him. 'Please don't say that. It just seemed so heavy, I didn't know how to do it.'

'But I'm your friend now, aren't I?' He raised his

hand and pushed my hair back from my face. 'Please tell me things.'

'Mmmm.' I reached up to kiss him and then whispered in his ear: 'I'll tell you something right now. It's taken us fifteen minutes to see Tilda and the baby to her car.'

We ran into the building.

I walked home by myself as Randal had to go to his French tutor's, another part of his parents' assault on his inability to speak French, despite having studied the language for several years.

So I strolled along, swinging my bag and feeling, now that I'd shared my secret with Randal and Tilda, almost light-hearted. Besides that, I was happy to have seen Jimmy's pleasure in his family. Perhaps even I might have a proper family one day. Just because I was an artist, it didn't mean I had to suffer all my life.

'Hello, Iris.' Aly had come up beside me. She answered my unspoken question. 'Janine's gone for a singing lesson.'

'Mr Stoller's a great teacher,' I said, non-committally.

'I told Janine that you wouldn't mind her going to Mr Stoller, but she wouldn't let me tell anyone. She's very shy.'

Oh yeah, I thought. So shy she can stand up and sing my song in front of everyone. I decided that anything I said would come out bitchier than I intended, so I changed the subject.

'Your patchwork blanket was beautiful.'

'But nothing like your gran's shawl! That was in a class of its own.'

We walked along the familiar street in silence. There was now so much that Aly didn't know about me, and she, similarly, had become a stranger. I did know that she spent a lot of time at Janine's, helping with the cooking and housework, because while Janine's mum was making a good recovery, she was still weak. I supposed that being a little helper was a better outlet for Aly's goodness than trying to reform one headstrong Leo.

Then, while I was still trying to think of something friendly to say, I realized that we'd reached my gate.

''Bye,' said Aly. 'See you later.'

'Yes, see you,' I said. And I watched Aly trip away, taking her usual tiny steps, until she was out of sight.

Chapter Sixteen

Our plans for the Fringe were going well. Jimmy had booked a hall for the second week of the Festival, and Adrian's aunt, who lived in Edinburgh, had found a neighbour who was willing to rent us her large house fairly cheaply because she'd be away on holiday at the time.

This was great news because if we saved on accommodation, we could spend more on publicity. With so many shows competing for attention, we'd need to work hard to get an audience.

However, Morven's mum and Rachel had both had good ideas. As the Scottish schools go back sooner than we do, Mrs Normansby was going to send special offer booking forms to local schools, advertising *Anaesthesia* as an educational experience. And then, because Dr Simpson, Adrian's character, had been an Edinburgh folk hero, Rachel suggested we print posters headed: 'WERE YOUR GREAT-GRANDPARENTS DELIVERED BY DR SIMPSON?' and put them up all over the suburbs to encourage people who wouldn't normally attend the festival to come to our show.

On the day we'd had the terrific news about the house I hurried home in a really good mood. I was to meet Randal after his French lesson, and then we were going to play tennis with Rachel and William. I'd never previously been the sporty type, but Randal was having this unexpected effect on me. Actually, I think the only reason he liked tennis was because he fancied himself in a white shirt and wristbands.

I bounced into the hall, dropped my bag, and went straight to the kitchen for a drink.

Maggie was sitting there with a glass of whisky in her hand and the bottle in front of her on the table. I'd been moving so fast that I was halfway to the fridge before I'd properly taken in her presence, and the amazing fact that she was drinking whisky at half past four in the afternoon.

She looked at me in a dazed sort of way, as though I were an unexpected guest. 'Ah, Iris,' she said eventually, remembering my name.

I sat down because I suddenly couldn't stand any longer. I had a terrible feeling that I wasn't going to like whatever was about to happen next. But at least I wouldn't let it hurt me.

'Iris,' she said, taking a long sip of her drink and then returning the glass carefully to the table. She had hung her jacket over the back of her chair, but her cream silk shirt had an untucked, rumpled look about it. She let her gaze wander round the kitchen before focusing, finally, upon me again.

I seemed to remind her of something. 'Iris. Oh yes. While you were at the farm I thought about what you said, and I agree with you, you do have some rights. You should at least be allowed to meet your father. So I wrote to him. I only received his reply today. He is quite definite that he wants no contact with you.'

Maggie said all this in a very rehearsed, unemotional way. When I made no reply, she continued: 'He says that his wife was always faithful to him, both before and after their marriage, and that if she knew he had betrayed her, it would break her heart. He also says that he has a daughter who would be traumatized if she found out the truth about his past. So he refused to meet you when you go to Edinburgh, either this year, or any time in the future.'

I tipped back my chair. 'They sound *distressingly* uptight to me,' I said. 'I don't *want* to know them.'

'Oh, Iris,' said Maggie. 'I'm glad you're taking this so well.' She put both hands on the table and twirled her glass round, first one way, and then the other. While she did this, she watched the procedure as if it were the most fascinating thing she'd ever seen. 'I didn't mean this to happen. I was wrong in not telling you sooner.'

'No, you weren't,' I said. 'You were quite right. We don't need him.'

'Do you really think so?'

Our eyes met across the table, and we both looked swiftly away.

'I can't tell you his name. Anyway, you'd only get hurt if you went looking for him.'

'It doesn't matter. I don't want to know.'

Maggie went back to fiddling with her glass. 'I'm so thankful you're being sensible about this. I've been worrying all day about telling you. As you can see.' She gestured towards the whisky. 'Perhaps we could go out together tomorrow. Have dinner. And I saw the loveliest Art Deco lamp; it would look wonderful in your room.'

When I didn't bother to reply, Maggie got up, collecting her glass in one hand and the bottle in the other. 'I think I'll just lie down for a little while. I'll see you later, pet.' And she left the room, taking very neat, precise steps.

I stood up and wandered round the kitchen. I

supposed that I was upset, but I didn't quite know how to do it. Eventually I left a note on the table, saying I'd gone round to Randal's, and quietly left the house.

It was a beautiful afternoon. I started off automatically in the direction of Randal's house, walking between gardens which were full of late daffodils and early white blossom.

Then I looked at my watch and realized, with a shock, that only ten minutes had passed since I'd arrived home, and that Randal would still be at his tutor's. It was probably just as well. I might frighten him away for ever if I turned up in this weird state.

I walked aimlessly towards the main road, thinking that perhaps I'd just stroll round in circles for a bit. I had my hands in my pockets, and after a while I noticed that I was folding and unfolding a bit of paper which I'd found in one of them. I took it out and recognized the scrap of notepaper which Tilda had written her address on. Although I'd wanted to visit her, I'd felt too shy to actually do it. I held up the paper, trying to make out her scrawly italic, and a taxi drew up beside me.

I knew, of course, that the driver had thought I was hailing him, but his prompt appearance seemed like some sort of sign, so I jumped in and gave him Tilda's address. Fortunately, Maggie insists that I always carry money for a taxi, so I knew that I should have enough in my purse to cover the fare to Islington.

We eventually arrived in a street of tall, narrow houses, similar to Wyn's, but scruffier. I paid the driver, went up the steps, and rang the bell. I knew from something Jimmy had once said that they lived in a communal house, so I wasn't surprised when the door was opened by a woman in a full-length denim dress and patchwork waistcoat, with her hair done in one long braid. In fact, she was exactly the sort of housemate I would've expected them to have.

She didn't seem in the least put out by the appearance of a distracted schoolgirl, but told me that Tilda was upstairs, first door on the right.

If I'd been in a different sort of mood, I would've enjoyed looking at Jimmy and Tilda's home, but as it was I just gained an impression of chipped white paint and plants and posters.

I knocked on the door and went in. Tilda was lying on a long sofa, reading the *Guardian*, with Dorinda asleep in her basket at her feet. When she saw me she sat up in surprise. 'How nice! I thought you weren't going to come – Iris, what's wrong?'

Her voice changed when she saw my face, and I realized that I must look as odd and spaced-out as I felt. I crossed the room and sat down beside her.

'My mother had a letter from my father today. She wrote and told him I was coming to Edinburgh, but he doesn't want to see me.' I found that I was speaking in the same flat tone that Maggie had used.

'But that's terrible! How can he?' Tilda actually sounded more upset than I did.

I explained about his wife and daughter. Until I said the words it hadn't actually got through to me that I had a half-sister. My voice began to shake. 'Just think of it, Tilda, I've got a half- sister and I'm not allowed to meet her! I told Maggie I didn't care, but I do! Why won't he meet me even once? I'm not so horrible, am I?'

Tilda put her arm round me. 'It's not you, love, of course you're not horrible. Perhaps he treated your mother badly and now he feels guilty.'

I remembered that I hadn't told Tilda the whole

story, so I explained about my father's engagement, and how Maggie had more or less stolen me from him.

Tilda tightened her arm round me. 'No wonder your father feels guilty. He sounds like the sort of person who sets himself up as perfect, so of course he can't cope when something like this catches him up. He must be terrified of losing his family's good opinion. His wife and daughter could probably deal with you perfectly well once they'd got over the shock, but he couldn't.'

'Do you think so?'

'Of course. It's nothing to do with you, truly; it's his problem, not yours.'

I wiped my eyes. I'd been determined not to cry, but it seemed impossible not to. 'It's just I hate him for not wanting me.'

I began to cry in earnest while Tilda hugged me and handed me tissues.

'Go on, you'll feel better if you cry,' she said, rocking me as though I were Dorinda. After a while, when I was sniffling instead of wailing, she said: 'But don't forget, your mother must've wanted you.'

'I suppose so,' I said, blowing my nose. 'Only, now she's got me, I have to be perfect. It's as though I'm proving something all the time. I'm proving that she was right to trick my father because I'm growing up into this educated, useful person. I mean, she'd feel awful if I grew up just to be a burden on the economy.'

'It feels like that just now, but in a few years it won't matter so much to you. You don't have to carry your parents round with you for ever.'

I sighed and looked at Dorinda, who was still fast asleep. 'Did you really want her? Oh!' I put my hand ver my mouth. 'I'm sorry, I shouldn't have said hat.'

Tilda laughed. 'Oh, don't worry, I was longing or a baby! I don't know why, I'd never wanted one efore.'

'Perhaps because you're married.'

'But married to Jimmy? Never any money, and otally impossible!' She dropped her little hands nto her lap and smiled, as though remembering vays in which Jimmy was impossible.

I asked something I'd been longing to know. How did you and Jimmy meet?'

'At college. I had the most terrible crush on him, ut I thought he'd never notice me because I was uch a mouse compared to the acting students. Then a whole bunch of us went to Paris, and one ight he and I got lost on the Métro: we got off at he wrong stop, and we've somehow been together ver since.'

I remembered the day I'd met Randal in Camden Market and decided that it was almost as romantic s an encounter on the Métro.

I must've been transparent because Tilda said: What about Randal? Are you in love with him?'

I hesitated. 'Well, I do love him, Tilda, but I'm ot sure if that's the same thing.' I could hardly say hat it was Jimmy with whom I'd once been in love. You see, Randal's so different from the way he ppears. Underneath all that laziness and silliness e's so sweet and kind-hearted, but he doesn't like o show it.'

'You'll just have to tempt him out of his hell, bit by bit—' Tilda was interrupted by a iny snuffling noise from Dorinda's basket. 'Oh no, he starts so quietly, but in a moment she'll be creaming.'

Tilda got up, gathered Dorinda into her arms and sat down in the chair opposite me. Sur enough, Dorinda's cries were rapidly becomin louder and louder.

'I was saying,' said Tilda, unbuttoning her shirt 'what you should do with Randal is—'

The door opened and Randal and Jimmy walke into the room. Tilda and I stared at Randal, an Jimmy stared at me. Then we all spoke at once.

I said: 'Randal, what are you doing here?'

Randal said to Jimmy: 'You see, she is here.' An then, to me: 'What happened? Are you all right?'

Jimmy said: 'Why is my child crying? Why is m home full of teenagers?'

Tilda said: 'Shut up, Jimmy, can't you see tha Iris has had a shock?'

Then Tilda pushed poor Dorinda up under he shirt, and there was immediate silence. We al looked at one another to see who was going to star speaking first.

Randal won. He came and sat beside me on th sofa, repeating: 'Are you all right, love?'

I was so pleased and surprised to see him that fell into his arms like the sort of wet movie heroin I most despise. 'How did you know I was here?'

'Your mother phoned up because she though you were at our house, and when I said you weren't she freaked out and said you'd had a scene and sh didn't know where else you might be. But I guesse you'd come here, so I looked up the address in th phone book, and here I am.'

I tilted my head back so that I could see hi face. He was looking simultaneously concerned an smug, but I forgave the smugness because I was s glad he'd come looking for me.

'Do you mean your mother doesn't know wher

you are?' said Tilda. 'You'd better phone her right away.'

She waved her free hand towards the phone, which was on the table by her side.

'Oh, I can't,' I said. 'Please.'

Tilda looked at me. 'OK, I'll do it.'

While she was talking to Maggie and assuring her that I was all right and would be home soon, Jimmy sank down onto the rug.

'I'm not old enough for this. Perhaps by the time Dorinda's fourteen or so I'll be able to deal with weeping teenagers after a hard day's work.' He leant back against the sofa. 'I'm only teasing. You know I'm honoured to have you come here and cry. Now please tell us what's wrong, sweetheart, or Randal and I will expire of worry and curiosity.'

I began to tell the story all over again, but now that I was surrounded by people being nice to me, it didn't seem to matter so much.

When I'd finished, Jimmy said: 'The bastard. He doesn't know what he's missing.'

Randal didn't say anything, but he held me more tightly.

'I don't care,' I said. 'I don't want to know him.'

'Let him go,' said Jimmy. He reached up and patted my feet. 'Imagine you're walking along a stormy beach. Just toss him into the wind. Let him blow away. Try it. It really works.'

'Really?'

'Would I lie to you?' He got up. 'I think we all need some coffee. Or tea? Hot chocolate even? Iris, what would you like?'

Hot chocolate always seems a rather babyish drink, but now it was just what I needed. I started to sit up. 'Chocolate, please. I'll help you.'

'No, you won't. You're a guest in distress. Lie

down on my nice sofa and allow yourself to be waited on hand and foot.'

'That's right,' said Randal. 'Do as you're told.'

I was actually glad to lie down with my head on Randal's knee because I really felt very peculiar, as though I'd cried myself as hollow as a Crunchie bar.

I shut my eyes. Randal was stroking my hair and talking to Tilda, but the conversation seemed very far away, like voices booming at the far end of an enormous cavern.

I imagined that I was walking down the empty Norfolk beach, throwing a tiny image of my father up into the wind. I saw him in a dark business suit and a tartan tie, spinning over and over, head over heels, disappearing for ever into the spray . . . I realized that I'd drifted off to sleep for a few minutes.

Randal was saying, in reply to a question of Tilda's: 'I fancied Iris for ages, but she used to go out with this repulsive Jean-Paul.'

I opened my eyes. 'You knew I was awake.'

'No, it was a test. I knew you were asleep and that you'd wake up whenever you heard your name.'

'Well, if it was a test, have I passed or failed?'

'Failed, of course. You've just proved that, even asleep, you're dozens of times vainer than the average person.

'Next time we're alone, I'll kill you.'

'I can hardly wait.'

Before this childish bickering could go any further Jimmy came in with a tray. He had obviously been out to a deli because, besides our drinks, he'd brought a selection of baklava, strudel, and Greek shortbread.

'Well, there's one thing,' he said, as he handed me my chocolate and a plate, 'when you've got your name in lights, your poor father won't be able to take any credit. He'll be kicking himself.'

I began to laugh. 'Do you know, that's exactly what I was thinking!'

'Yes, there he'll be, having a snifter with his stuffy Scottish colleagues, and they'll all be saying, "Have you seen yon lovely lassie who's starring at the Festival Theatre?" and he'll be longing to say, "Thon's ma wee gurrrrl," but his lips will be sealed for ever over his guilty secret!'

'Don't, Jimmy,' said Tilda, but Randal and I were rolling about with laughter at Jimmy's atrocious Scottish accent.

He went on and on, making up ever more fantastic stories about my imaginary parent. He wore hairy tartan underpants. He grew thistles for a hobby. He made his family eat porridge for every meal.

'Stop, Jimmy,' I said eventually. 'I can't laugh any more.'

'I'll spare you,' he said. 'After all, we need you for *Anaesthesia* – oh God, you are still coming, aren't you?' He looked genuinely alarmed.

'Of course I am! Do you think I'd let that stop me?'

'The Iris I know and love.'

'Come on,' said Randal. 'I'd better take you home. I've got my mother's car.'

'She let you have her car!'

Randal passed his test before Christmas, but his parents are both very protective of their cars.

'I told her it was an emergency.'

We got up to go. Tilda hugged me and told me to come again soon, and Jimmy came down to see us off.

'Thank you, Jimmy,' I said. 'I'm sorry I've been such a nuisance.'

He hugged me, as Tilda had done. 'Don't worry. We'll make you pay in baby-sitting. Now take her away, Randal, please.'

Randal unlocked the door for me and I climbed into his mother's huge Volvo, the back of which was piled high with wallpaper books and fabric samples. Then he leaned across and took my hand. 'Feeling better?'

I nodded, and took the risk of embarrassing us both. 'Thank you for coming to find me,' I said.

He grinned at me. 'What choice did I have? I'd be lost without you.'

Chapter Seventeen

'Now, if you look to the north of Princes Street, you can see how the Georgian part of the city sweeps down to the sea in spacious streets and crescents, quite unlike the higgledy-piggledy old town—'

The freezing cold wind, which had been blowing ever since we arrived in Edinburgh over a week ago, whisked away Mrs Reilly's words. It was the morning after our first night, and a few of us were huddled together on the summit of Calton Hill, a tiny peak right in the centre of the city. We all had different reasons for being there at 11.30 on a Sunday morning. Some serious people, like Rachel and Aly, actually wanted to hear Mrs Reilly, our art teacher and wardrobe mistress, enthuse over the beauties of historic Scotland. Morven, as the only one of us to have been here before, wanted to go on showing off her knowledge of the city. And I, of course, had a morbid desire to see as much of Edinburgh as possible, in case my father and stepmother and unknown little sister lived in one of these tiny, grey, distant houses.

Randal had nobly come to keep me company. 'Thank God I brought grandfather's coat,' he said. 'Look at that – the sun's coming out but the wind's as cold as ever.'

I wished I had my faux fur. It was so cold that

I'd been obliged to buy an Aran sweater, a garment I've always considered less than chic, but at least it was now keeping me cosy.

I leant against Randal and sighed. 'He could be anywhere.'

He knew whom I meant. 'It's not worth worrying about, it's so unlikely that you'll just run into him – especially as he knows you're here.'

'Yes. Maggie told him in her letter when I was coming, so I dare say he's gone underground and taken his family with him.'

'He'd hardly need to bother. If your mum had known how crowded Edinburgh is during the festival, she wouldn't have worried about your meeting.'

It was true. The centre of the tiny city, with its narrow, grey, cobbled streets and elegant gardens, was absolutely packed with the most interesting selection of people I'd ever seen. The dowdy Edinburghers were totally out-numbered by exotic visitors – wonderful foreign women in designer clothes, troupes of New Age travellers selling jewellery and hair braids, jugglers, acrobats, musicians, people in every sort of national costume . . . Randal was right. I'd never stumble across my father or my little sister. And even if I did, I had no way of recognizing them.

I sighed again.

'I wish you weren't so unhappy about it.'

It was true that I was unhappy. After the big scene at Tilda's everything had, at first, seemed so much better. Randal hadn't actually run away in terror because he'd seen me crying. Tilda had insisted that I visit her again, and Jimmy had almost stopped shouting at me during rehearsals. Even Maggie and I had managed to maintain our truce, and had tried not to irritate one another. Neither of us had mentioned my father again until the night before I left. I'd looked up from my packing to see Maggie standing in the doorway.

'You do understand why I can't tell you his name?' she said. 'I would tell you if it were up to me.'

'I told you, I don't care.'

But now that I was here, in Edinburgh, it seemed to matter all over again, and the knowledge that there was someone here, in the city, who absolutely didn't want to see me took the edge off all my usual pleasure in acting and singing.

But things were difficult for everybody, not just me. Despite the rehearsal time we'd had before we left London, the show had somehow fallen apart in the new venue. We had fewer musicians, and Mrs Reece had to coax them into making a fuller sound. Some of the re-casting was causing problems, the chorus numbers had to be altered for the smaller stage, and our acting seemed to be either stale or over-dramatic. Jimmy swore at us in vain, and at the stage crew, who had to work even harder than we did, adjusting scenery and lights. And when we weren't rehearsing we were either running errands for Mrs Reilly or a frantic stage manager, or putting up posters with Mrs Normansby in the dismal Scottish rain.

By the time the first night actually came, it was amazing that we were able to give a performance at all. But Jimmy's teaching and our hard work paid off, and we somehow got through the show without any real disasters. It was hardly our most sparkling effort, but at least we'd done it.

All that remained now was to get back some of the zest we'd had at Christmas – and to attract bigger houses. We'd been disappointed that the hall was barely half full, although Jimmy and Tilda assured us that that was really good for the first night of an unknown Fringe show.

'A lot of school parties are coming,' said Jimmy, 'and the street theatre should pull in more punters. And if we get a good review . . .'

A good review! We'd quickly learnt that every Fringe group dreamed of receiving a rave notice in one of the quality papers, just a few words which would attract the attention of a possible audience. Jimmy, however, despite our pleas, refused to say whether or not he knew if a critic were coming to see us.

'It shouldn't make any difference to the quality of your performance,' he had said dismissively. 'A real pro always gives his or her best.'

Well, so far, our best had been pretty feeble, and those of us who were standing on the chilly hill-top had probably all come because we were feeling a bit flat and unsettled, as well as for our own private reasons. But if we'd hoped that Mrs Reilly's cultural expedition would take our minds off the show, we were mistaken.

'I just hope the houses get bigger,' said Rachel, who had no more been listening to Mrs Reilly than had Randal and I.

'So do I,' I said, forcing my thoughts away from my own problems. 'It's so depressing, playing to only a handful of people.'

Aly, who was actually there without Janine, who had waited behind for a phone call from her mother, tried to console us. 'Remember that a lot of school parties are coming.'

'Did I tell you,' said Morven, 'when I was here before I met this fantastic boy who went to the most exclusive school in Edinburgh and—' Glancing at Mrs Reilly, she lowered her voice.

Aly caught my eye, and she and Randal and I giggled. For a moment it was almost as though we were all walking home together again. Then the wind veered round and unexpectedly blew Morven's description of her exploits towards Mrs Reilly, who, wrapping herself more tightly in her highly artistic, hand-woven shawl, said: 'Ah, Morven, as you're so well versed in Scottish geography, you can show us the way to the nearest bus stop before we all freeze to death.'

Morven snapped her little mouth shut and set off at high speed down one of the asphalt paths, while Mrs Reilly, like an exceptionally elegant sheepdog, herded the rest of us in her wake.

The bus, once we'd climbed aboard, edged slowly along the spectacularly beautiful Princes Street, with its gardens on one side, and above the gardens, the amazing castle, perched on a theatrical rock. If it had been a stage set, no-one would've believed it.

'Look,' said Morven, who had recovered her usual self-importance, 'there's where we'll be performing tomorrow.' She pointed out of the window.

In between the gardens, at the foot of the castle hill, was a large paved area. From our viewpoint on the top of the bus we could see over the crowd to where a group in elaborate Japanese costume were dancing, while, on the other side of the square, three men were juggling on skateboards.

'It'll be difficult to attract a crowd with so much competition,' said Sarah gloomily. She looked colder than the rest of us in a tiny silk jacket and low-cut T-shirt.

'I don't think so,' said Morven. 'When we were

here before I noticed that the crowds really loved seeing young performers. I remember that there was this amazing group who . . .'

I leant back against Randal, who was comfortably upholstered in his tweed, and watched the city go by.

I'd been assuming that my father, like Maggie, was successful and well-paid, but perhaps he hadn't made it. Perhaps he didn't live in a large house, but in one of the forbidding tenements which lined our route. Maybe my sister went down to that very corner shop, which we were passing now, to buy chocolate and her copy of *Just 17*.

Randal shook me. 'Wake up – our stop.'

In my daydream I hadn't noticed that we'd reached the respectable Victorian suburb where we were staying. Our street, in fact, was very similar to the ones in which many of us lived at home, although the actual houses were much more elaborate, being adorned with turrets and spires and battlements like a row of miniature castles. Our house was totally crazy – vaguely like an Italian villa at the front, all columns and balconies, but with two little fairytale turrets stuck on at the back.

We all loved it, not least because it was centrally heated and beautifully warm, and we now raced in after our outing, feeling self-righteous and healthy. We might still be depressed about the show, but at least we hadn't stayed at home moping like the others.

Dinah had heard us and came bounding down the stairs. 'What do you think? Janine's mum can come to the show after all!'

We all knew that she'd been longing to come, but had been afraid that the journey, and then staying in a busy hotel, would be too tiring.

'Adrian's mum's coming, and she's persuaded Mrs Boswell to come with her. They're going to fly up and stay with Adrian's aunt – that's the one who found us this house – so there'll be no hassle with driving or finding a hotel.'

'Isn't it wonderful?' Janine had appeared behind Dinah, her face glowing. She looked prettier than I'd ever seen her. 'She's coming tomorrow night. And I thought she might never see it!'

Everyone was aware that there was a darker meaning behind her words, and there was a tiny silence.

'That's fantastic!' Aly said quickly, rushing forward. 'Are you going round to meet her? When are they arriving?'

They scurried off together while everyone else headed for the kitchen.

I sank down onto the foot of the curved staircase. 'Oh, hell! Damn. Rats. I'll have to do it.' The moment I'd seen Janine looking so happy, I'd known what I needed to do.

'Do what?' Randal sat down beside me.

'OK. Who has the bigger part, me or Janine?'

'You do.'

'Who has two solos, me or Janine?'

'You do.'

'Whose mother is coming tomorrow, mine or Janine's?'

'Janine's.'

'And who's my understudy?'

'Oh come on, Iris, why should you? And Jimmy wouldn't let you.' Randal leant back against the wall and stretched his legs out in front of him.

'I don't see why not. She's a better actress than I am. Anyway, I've got to ask him. Don't you see?'

'Not really,' he said.

This wasn't the response I wanted. 'Well, it's like this book I read when I was about ten. The heroine is understudying the lead in a big show. One day she learns that the kids from her old school are coming to a performance and—'

'Don't tell me, the leading actress lets the understudy go on.'

'Exactly.'

'I think you're crazy. You're not ten now, you're seventeen, though no-one would think it from the way you carry on.'

I'd been really disappointed that my birthday had fallen before the festival, but I'd had a party at William's house because his parents are very laid back about raves in their basement, and because William had passed his driving test and wanted to celebrate too. Randal, despite his present mean remarks, had given me a beautiful pair of ear-rings, huge chunks of pale amber in silver settings. I was actually wearing them now – in fact, I'd worn them every day since he gave them to me – and they swung lightly as I tossed my head.

'Honestly, Randal, I thought you might've been more supportive.'

'I'm not stopping you.'

'As if I'd let you!'

I'd expected more encouragement from Randal, so I got up huffily and went in search of Jimmy. I hated to think of Janine singing my music, but then, when I imagined how thrilled and moved her mother would be at the sight of Janine in my lilac dress, warbling in the spotlight, the sacrifice seemed almost worthwhile.

I finally tracked Jimmy down to the turret room, which he and Tilda shared with Dorinda and all her baby bits and pieces. He was sitting on the bed, surrounded by scripts and paper and coloured pens. When he saw me he waved his hand impatiently at the drifts of scrawled-upon paper.

'What does this look like? Work. Yes, even to your untrained eye, it must be apparent that I am working. Go away.'

It's impossible to be afraid of someone when you have wept on their sofa.

'I'll only be a minute, Jimmy. Listen, do you remember when Janine's mother couldn't come to the show?'

'How could I forget?'

'Well, the thing is, she's coming *tomorrow*, so I thought, well, how would it be if Janine played my part tomorrow so that her mum could hear her sing?'

Jimmy sighed. He lay back against the pillows and closed his eyes. Then he opened them and said: 'Iris. The ultimate sacrifice.'

'What?'

'The noble gesture. It's a nice idea, but I can't let you do it. It would unbalance the entire casting of the play. Janine would act the part as well as you – perhaps even better – but she doesn't have your singing voice, or your height, or, to be honest, your looks, so she wouldn't create the same impression. And then Melanie wouldn't be half as good as Janine in her part, and the chorus would be weaker without Melanie's voice. See?'

'But just for one night?' I was very reluctant to give up my good deed.

'I wasn't going to tell anyone until before the show, so keep this to yourself, but a friend of mine has promised to come tomorrow.'

'What sort of friend? A journalist?'

'Let's just say that I want tomorrow's

performance to be a cracker, so don't do anything clever like pretending you've sprained your ankle or lost your voice. Do I make myself clear?'

'Yes, Jimmy.' Jimmy hadn't sounded so angry with me for a long time.

'And one more thing: I'm not encouraging you to become hard, but keep your generosity for your private life. If you really intend going into the theatre, you'll have to be tougher. You can't give up a juicy part, even for one performance, because you want to be *nice*, or people will walk all over you. Understand?'

I felt very stupid and schoolgirlish. 'Yes. I'm sorry to have bothered you.'

'And remember, not a word about my – mmm – friend.'

'Yes, Jimmy, I mean, not a word.' I opened the door.

'Iris.'

I stopped.

'It was a sweet thing to do.'

I felt myself becoming pink, but before I could escape he said: 'Tell me something else, love, are you fretting about your father?'

I turned round swiftly. 'It's not affecting my work, is it?'

'No, no, relax, not at all. Just remember that other people appreciate you, OK?'

I more or less danced down the stairs and found Randal sitting exactly where I'd left him.

'You're looking very pleased with yourself.'

'I asked him, but he said no.'

'There you are, what did I tell you? But at least you've had all the glory of offering to do good, without the hassle of putting it into practice.'

I sat down heavily on his knee. 'Randal, I hate you.'

'I know you do,' he said complacently. 'I wish this house were less full of people, then we could find a quiet corner and you could tell me just how much.'

Chapter Eighteen

It was exhilarating singing out of doors next day. The fiendish wind had dropped in time for our street performance, and the sunshine was almost warm on our faces as we sang and danced through a selection of our big numbers. And it even seemed that Morven had been right, for despite competition from a South American folk group, a juggler, and a bunch of students singing in First World War uniform, we drew a large crowd. We particularly appealed to older Americans, who thought it cute that kids should be doing a show, and to local people, who were still proud of the memory of Dr Simpson.

When we'd finished singing, we all took bundles of flyers and handed them out to the crowd.

'Look over there.' Dinah nudged my arm. 'That girl's got hair exactly the same colour as yours.'

Despite myself, I whirled round at her words, heart thumping.

Sure enough, a few paces away from us stood a girl of about twelve in a school uniform of blue blazer and pleated tartan skirt. Her shoulder-length hair was precisely the same shade of dark chestnut as mine. However, as she turned towards us, I saw that she didn't resemble me at all. Instead of my long, slanting, dark-eyed face, she had a pointed chin, light-blue eyes, and a turned-up nose. The red hair hadn't meant anything. After all, lots of Scottish people had red hair.

The girl, though, was looking at me, so I smiled and offered her a flyer.

She shook her head. 'I've seen it already,' she said, in a funny, precise, Scottish accent. 'I went last night with the school. I thought you were wonderful.' She was regarding me with real admiration.

'I'm glad you enjoyed it,' I said, flattered to get a compliment from a genuine, paying customer.

'It's the best thing I've seen at the festival so far, and to think I almost missed it! My father didn't want me to go.'

'Why not?' I asked curiously. 'Doesn't he approve of the theatre?' Perhaps parents up here were really stuffy and old-fashioned.

'He usually loves it, so I don't know what got into him. He was absolutely furious with the school for booking the tickets without checking with the parents first, but in the end he had to let me go because I'm doing a project on the history of medicine in Edinburgh.' She chattered on, looking really thrilled to be talking to a performer.

'How odd,' I said, as calmly as possible. 'My mum didn't want me to do this show in the first place.'

'What a coincidence. Our parents sound really alike.'

I became aware that Dinah had drifted away, and that Randal was standing beside me. He took my hand and I knew that we were thinking the same thing. I held onto him tightly.

'Yes, they do,' I said carefully. 'I wonder if there are any other similarities. My mum's in fashion. What does your father do?'

'How weird!' cried the girl, throwing up her hands so that a bunch of silver bracelets ran up her arm. 'Dad's in fashion too! He's the manager of a knitwear firm. They make woollies for tiny tots – it's called the Crofter's Bairn.' She wrinkled up her little nose in disgust. 'Isn't that a daft name?'

'That's nothing,' I said. I could scarcely get out the next words, but years of breathing exercises helped. I took as deep a breath as my tight bodice would allow. 'My mum used to work for a firm called Truelove Lingerie.'

'But that's incredible! Dad used to work there. Years and years ago, before he and Mum got married.'

The calm part of me which helped me to act took over. 'What's your father's name?' I said. 'I must ask Mum if she remembers him.'

'Colin Blane. And my name's Verity.'

'Verity,' I repeated. 'And I'm—'

'Och, I know your name,' said Verity. 'I looked it up specially in the programme because I thought you were so good.' She grinned shyly. 'I'm so pleased to have met you.'

Then, as though embarrassed at having said so much, she added: 'I've got to go now, it's my lunch hour,' and she disappeared into the crowd.

She wore braces on her front teeth. I never thought I'd find *braces* touching.

'My God, Randal,' I said, 'it's got to be her, it's simply got to. You heard what she said. Maggie and her father worked in Truelove years ago, before he was married. And he tried to stop her seeing the show. And our hair! She's got to be my half-sister. I thought I was never going to see her, and we meet right here!'

'Calm down, Iris. You're right, I know you are, but Morven's mum is looking at you.'

'The most incredible moment of my entire life and you tell me to calm down!' I let go of Randal, at the same time dropping the leaflets which I held in my other hand. 'Don't you realize that I can find my father now? Maggie can't stop me.'

'Yes, of course you can find him, but keep your voice down, or everyone will know what's happened.' Randal was talking to me in an infuriating, soothing tone of voice, as though I were hysterical.

'I don't care if everyone hears me. Do you think I'm ashamed of having a father? Isn't everyone supposed to have a father?'

I was backing away from Randal, my crinoline brushing against passers-by, while Randal, pursuing me in Victorian clergyman's outfit, looked simultaneously handsome and ludicrous.

I suddenly wanted to laugh, which made me realize that Randal was right, and I was losing control.

I stopped retreating and let him put his arm round me. 'I have to have some coffee,' I said. 'I can't think until I've had a cup of coffee.'

'Come on, everyone else is halfway up the steps by now.' Tilda had come up quietly in her espadrilles, Dorinda slung across her breast. She gestured towards the long flight of steps which ran up the hill behind us.

Seeing her, I totally forgot about being calm. 'Listen, listen, Tilda, you won't believe it, but I've just met my *sister*! She was watching us. Her hair's just the same colour as mine, she's so sweet. Our parents worked together at Truelove.'

While I shook with impatience, Randal gave Tilda a more sensible account of what had happened. To my irritation, she then began to behave exactly like Randal.

'That's amazing, love. Let's sit down and talk about it. There's a café just over there.'

She put her hand through my other arm, and they led me past the stalls which lined the square and round the other performers, as though I were a dangerous escaped prisoner. When I realized what was happening, and how stupid I must look, I began doing my breathing exercises again.

'I'm sorry,' I said, when I felt a little less hyper. 'I was being silly. Now I'm totally in control.'

They both laughed at me, which made things feel more normal.

When we reached the outdoor café Tilda and I sat down while Randal fetched our coffees. Fortunately, there were so many peculiarly dressed people wandering about that our little group of a long-haired clergyman, a girl in a crinoline, and a woman in a flowing, embroidered smock and scarlet espadrilles, didn't look in the least odd.

Tilda untied Dorinda's sling and lowered her onto her knee. 'Tell me all over again,' she said. 'I don't think I've quite grasped it.'

Randal explained while I stirred spoonfuls of sugar into my *espresso. Cappuccino* had seemed too wimpish for the occasion.

'Surely the first thing to do is phone your mother,' said Tilda, behaving disappointingly like a proper grown-up.

'No,' I said. 'Maggie'll just say that I'm not to try and see him, but now that this has happened, I have to do *something*, I can't just sit around. It's like fate is calling me to action.'

'Well, you can hardly go barging into his office,' said Randal. 'What if you look really like him? All his staff would guess who you are.'

'But wait, wait,' said Tilda, 'you still don't know for sure that this man is your father and that Verity is your sister—'

'She *is*,' I said. 'I could feel it.'

I caught Randal and Tilda exchanging glances.

'Listen, Iris,' said Tilda, 'I think you should write to Mr Blane. Tell him that meeting Verity was a complete accident, but that now it's happened you think that you and he should meet. And you can add that, if you're mistaken and you aren't related, you apologize for having disturbed him.'

'But what if he doesn't reply?'

'Then we think again.'

'Fine then, I'll do it right away.' Fired up with caffeine and adrenaline, I jumped to my feet. 'I'll go back to the house: I'll get a bit of peace and quiet there to write the letter.'

'But you'll have to go to the hall first to leave your costume,' pointed out Randal.

I waved my hands impatiently. The thought of walking four blocks to the hall, changing into my jeans, and making some excuse to Mrs Normansby for being late, was too much for me. The sooner I posted the letter, the sooner I might get a reply!

Tilda was watching me. 'Here's what we'll do. Iris, you and I'll get a taxi back to the house, and Randal, you find Jimmy and tell him I've gone home to feed Dorinda and Iris has come with me to keep me company. Don't say a word to him about this – he's on edge enough about Justin coming tonight—' She hesitated, and I realized that she'd almost let slip Jimmy's secret about the critic's visit. 'Justin is an old friend of ours, and Jimmy really wants to impress him,' she finished. 'Just don't give him anything else to think about.'

Needless to say, I'd completely forgotten that this was the night when we had to give the show everything we'd got. I hoped that, by the evening, I'd still have enough energy left to go on the stage, let alone give a scintillating performance.

Tilda was looking at me anxiously, and I could tell that she was thinking the same thing. 'Perhaps you ought to lie down for a bit after you've written your letter,' she said. 'I know Jimmy wants everyone to do their best tonight.'

I drew myself up. 'Really, Tilda, you don't need to worry. I *am* an actress.'

A couple of hours later, having gone through several drafts of the letter, copied out the most coherent one, and rushed with it to the nearest postbox – just in time to catch a collection – I hoped that I hadn't been wrong in saying that, come what may, I would give my best possible performance that evening.

I was absolutely exhausted. Tilda had told me to lie down in their room, as she and Jimmy were going out with Justin and I wouldn't be disturbed. I shut my eyes and hoped that the effects of the coffee had died down enough to allow me to sleep.

Then I thought of something so terrible that my eyes flew open. If I couldn't go on tonight, my understudy would have to take my place! Janine! Jimmy would think I'd made myself ill on purpose. He'd never trust me again.

I began to panic. I had to get to sleep. I couldn't turn up for the show a trembling bag of nerves. What if I collapsed?

I clenched my fists. If only I could think of something calm and soothing – like my waterlily picture! I shut my eyes and let myself relax. Soon the huge pale blossoms seemed to be floating around my head, while the dark-blue water supported me . . . in a few moments, I was fast asleep.

Chapter Nineteen

'Jimmy's so sly – fancy not telling us until just five minutes before curtain up!'

'I suppose he didn't want us to have time to be nervous.'

'Nervous! I'd rather not have known at all.'

'Do you think the crit'll come out tomorrow?'

'What if it's awful?'

'They're never really down on kids' shows. They say things like: "a brave attempt" or "a spirited performance".'

'I'd rather be slated than patronized!'

'But if it sells more seats?'

'Well, the house was pretty full tonight.'

About a dozen of us were sitting in the kitchen, going over and over this evening's performance.

The kitchen was my favourite room in the big house. The tables and cupboards, unlike those belonging to Maggie or to Randal's mum, were really old, and every inch of wall was covered by fabulous paintings done by the little kids who usually lived here.

Whenever I was in this kitchen, I thought how great it would be to have one just like it. Of course, if I were going to act and sing *and* have children, I'd need a good nanny. And if Verity came to stay, we'd do stuff together with the kids—

'You were really acting well tonight, Iris,' I heard Adrian say, the sound of my name bringing me back to earth. 'When you were begging for my help tonight, I really believed you.'

I tried not to look ridiculously pleased, but I was, because Adrian hardly ever praises anyone. Like Jimmy, he has very high standards – for himself as well as for other people.

'But you make it easy,' I said with perfect sincerity. 'You always believe what you're doing, so I've only got to look at you to be serious too.'

'But it doesn't always work as well as it did tonight.'

I knew he was speaking the truth. Despite everything, I'd managed to pull myself together and hang on to Effie's emotions and not my own. I'd woken up still feeling spaced-out, but Randal had brought me a cup of coffee and a sandwich, and by the time I'd got to the hall and into my dress, my surroundings seemed only a little woolly and peculiar, rather than at an immense distance. In fact, it was almost a repeat of the first night, when I used my fear to fuel Effie's.

'Did your mum enjoy the show, Janine?'

Janine, who was sitting on the window seat, brushing out her ringlets, turned to answer Dinah. 'She loved it. And I'm so pleased she got to see me in a part which suits me. I mean, I couldn't sing every night like you, Iris. I'd be petrified. Please don't fall ill, whatever you do. It was the worst moment of my life when Jimmy made me your understudy.'

'Really?' I said weakly.

'Yes. When I auditioned, I thought he might give me a nursery rhyme or something. I could never sing your songs!'

Randal, who was leaning against the sink, smirked horribly.

I turned my back on him. 'But I couldn't possibly play *your* part,' I said to Janine. 'I could never be funny like you can.'

'So things couldn't have worked out better,' said Randal. 'You're perfect as Effie and Janine's perfect as Jessie.'

'I'm going to bed,' I said. I thought I'd better leave the room before I leapt upon Randal and drowned him in the sink. I hated to be reminded of the embarrassing scene with Jimmy. Why on earth had I offered to let Janine play my part? The fact that she didn't want it made me feel still worse – even though Jimmy had been so nice about it.

I said goodnight and left the room. Randal, as I expected, came padding upstairs behind me.

'Promise you won't tell anyone that I offered to let Janine go on. Please.'

'Your secret is safe with me. For the present. I'm not promising that I won't blackmail you later.'

I stopped on the landing. 'You're being so mean about it! I was only trying to be *nice*.'

'I know, but it's so upsetting to have you behaving out of character.'

I spun round and slapped him so hard that I actually hurt my hand. Then I was so horrified by what I'd done that I found I'd put my other hand over my mouth to muffle my own scream. 'I didn't mean to!' I cried. 'I didn't mean to!'

I stretched out my sore hand and, very gently, stroked his cheek. Now I'd ruined everything.

Randal didn't say a word.

I began to withdraw my hand, but he caught it and, looking into his face, I saw that his eyes were full of tears.

'I deserved it,' he said. 'I shouldn't have been teasing you. I know you're worrying about your father and whether you'll get to see your little sister again. I know you're upset, and I'm upset for you, but I just couldn't tell you, see? So I was teasing you.'

I thought at first his tears were because I'd hit him so hard, but I was wrong. He was actually ready to cry.

We put our arms round one another.

'I know,' I said. 'I know you didn't mean it. I just got carried away.'

'You had every right.' He buried his face in my hair, so I could hardly hear his next words. 'I wish I were more like you, Iris.'

I held him as tightly as I could. 'Oh, don't wish to be like me!'

'Yes I do! I wish I could say what I actually feel, instead of driving people wild by winding them up. You were right when you said I couldn't act because I was too scared of my feelings.'

I freed myself sufficiently to lean back and see his face. He began to wipe his eyes, but I stopped him.

'This is lesson one,' I said. 'See what crying feels like. Then it'll be easier to do it again.'

I eventually tore myself away from Randal and went to bed in the room which I shared with five of the other girls. I lay awake for a long time, alternately dreaming about Randal and worrying about my father's response to my letter.

The one thing I forgot about was the review.

I was woken up next morning by every other person in the room screaming and shrieking.

'Let me see – a photo! Fantastic!'

'What does it say?'
'Move over, Dinah, I can't see.'
'Wake up, Iris, we've got a crit!'
'And a *photo* – look at Adrian!'

I was awake in a flash and burrowing between Dinah and Morven to see the precious column. Jimmy's friend had written quite a long article, headed TOMORROW'S TALENT IN TODAY'S FRINGE, in which he compared four youth theatre groups.

'Look, there we are!' Dinah pointed to the word ANAESTHESIA in heavy print – and then gave an extra scream: 'Iris, he mentions you specially!'

I was finding it difficult to focus, but sure enough, there was my name:

> Blacklock's School Theatre Company is fortunate in having a compelling and varied score by Blake Evans, and Evans is well served by the enthusiastic cast, and especially by Iris Campion, who, as Effie, sings his music with a beauty of tone and accuracy of emotion unusual in so young a performer.

I fell back on Dinah's bed.

'He says Adrian gave "an impressive portrait of a complex medical hero".'

' "Highly unusual, but well-thought-out scenario" – there you are, Rachel!'

' ". . . tellingly comic Queen Victoria".'

'But look at you, Iris – "beauty of tone"!'

Last term Mr Stoller had taught me a passionate Spanish gypsy song because he said it suited my character. Now I leapt up and began to stamp and click my fingers, while uttering full-throated flamenco cries. He was right – nothing else could possibly have expressed how I felt at that moment.

Dinah and Rachel joined in, clapping their hands and shouting 'Olé!' with the result that William had to shout 'Phone!' several times before anyone heard him.

'Iris, it's for you.'

Maggie must have seen the paper! I skidded along the corridor towards the nearest phone, which was hidden away in a linen cupboard, and snatched up the receiver.

'Maggie, did you see the review?'

There was no reply. Then a male voice with a familiar, precise, Edinburgh accent said: 'Is this Iris Campion?'

I slid down the door jamb and came to rest on the cupboard floor.

'Yes,' I said.

'My name is Colin Blane. I've just received your letter.' He paused. 'In view of what happened yesterday, I think we should meet. Could you manage lunch today?'

Today!

'Yes,' I said again.

'I think this restaurant would be convenient for you.' He gave me a name and address. 'Would twelve-thirty suit you?'

'Yes.' I was hardly revealing myself as a brilliant conversationalist.

'Very well. Twelve-thirty.'

He put down the phone.

Chapter Twenty

Two and a half hours later I was walking down the nearest main road with Tilda, who had volunteered to come part of the way with me. Randal had refused to join us on the grounds that, if he saw my father, he'd be tempted to kill him for having made me miserable.

Jimmy, on a tremendous high after the review, had said something similar once I'd explained what had happened. 'If he doesn't do the decent thing by you, I'll throttle him with one of his own thistles. No, seriously, love, don't give him the power to hurt you. Remember, he's the one who's mixed up, not you.'

'I hope so.'

'Believe me, I'm the expert. And don't worry, you look wonderful.'

This was exactly what I needed to hear. I'd spent all morning taking on and off different outfits and re-doing my hair. Now I was wearing a long dark cotton dress, a black angora cardigan which I'd borrowed from Rachel and, of course, my amber ear-rings. I'd also put my hair up because I wanted to look respectable and dignified – the sort of person, in fact, whom a middle-aged businessman would be proud to have as his daughter.

'Are you sure I look all right?' I asked Tilda for about the tenth time since we'd left the house. I was so nervous that my appearance was all I could concentrate on. This probably meant that I was a pretty shallow person, and hardly, therefore, a desirable relative.

Then I said, again for the tenth time: 'The post's too efficient up here. I need more time.'

'Look,' said Tilda, 'that must be the restaurant.'

The road, which was steep and narrow, with the shops and people and traffic crowded between the usual towering grey tenements, opened out ahead of us. It grew broader and there was a dusty little park on the far side. Facing the park was the café where I was to meet my father.

'Would you like us to wait for you in that park?' Tilda, as usual, was carrying Dorinda.

'Do you mind?'

'Of course not! Go on. It's twelve-thirty.'

'I know.' I'd been looking at my watch every two seconds since we'd left.

Tilda kissed me. 'Go on. We'll be waiting.'

I checked my hair and dress and ear-rings for the last time, and walked into the little restaurant.

It could easily have been decorated by Randal's mother. There were flowery curtains looped over the windows, and vases of dried flowers on the pine tables, most of which were occupied by groups of old ladies. Had I made a mistake? It seemed a very unlikely place to meet a middle-aged man – but then, seeing one single male at a corner table, I understood. There was little danger of any of my father's friends seeing us in this out-of-the-way, cosy spot.

The man stood up. He was unmistakably my father.

I had his red hair and dark-blue eyes and high cheekbones, although my mouth, I now realized, was Maggie's, not his stern, tightly pressed together lips.

He came towards me. 'Iris?' He made no move to touch me. 'What would you like to eat?' He gestured towards the counter.

I couldn't imagine swallowing anything. 'Just some salad, please. And a glass of water.'

'I hope you're not a vegetarian.'

I couldn't believe that this was my father's first personal remark to me! I tried to take hold of myself. Probably he was as nervous as I was.

I carried my tray to the table and sat down facing him. He was wearing an expensively styled dark suit, a beautiful white shirt which certainly hadn't come from a chain store, and some sort of academic tie.

He, too, was looking at me, and I was glad that I'd gone to so much trouble over my appearance.

'I told your mother quite distinctly that you were not to contact me.'

I wished that he didn't have that affected Scottish accent. It made it difficult for me to take him seriously. And it was so weird to be discussing Maggie like this with a stranger.

'I know,' I said curtly. 'And as she gave me neither your name nor your address it would have been impossible for me to do so. As I told you in my letter, meeting Verity was a complete accident.'

I noticed that he winced when I said Verity's name. Perhaps I wasn't worthy to pronounce the sacred syllables? I told myself to keep cool. How would Maggie want me to behave? I realized that I'd scarcely thought about how this meeting would affect her. Would she be angry, or upset?

'However, during the short time you and Verity were together, you managed to extract from her my name and business address.'

How dare he be so pompous? What did he expect me to do?

I took a tiny mouthful of salad. As I was disobeying Maggie, the least I could do was behave in such a way as to make her proud of me. Whatever happened, I mustn't lose my temper.

'Yes,' I said calmly. 'I knew there was no chance of my mother telling me anything about you, so when I realized who Verity was, it was too good an opportunity to miss. Surely you can understand my being curious about you? But I've no intention of bothering you again, or of trying to see Verity without your permission.'

'And I've no intention of allowing you to see her again!' he said sharply.

I was right. The thought of his precious little girl and his bastard daughter meeting was completely repugnant to him.

He saw that he'd shocked me, and changed to a smooth, business-like tone, as though I were simply a difficult client. 'You must appreciate that my wife and daughter are entirely ignorant of your existence, and that your appearance would therefore place a strain upon our life together as a family.'

When I didn't reply, he continued: 'My wife has delicate health, and I would do anything to preserve her from a shock of this nature. The effect upon her could be very serious.'

I wondered if he always spoke in these elaborate old-fashioned sentences.

'As for Verity, she is only a child, and I appeal to you, Iris, to do nothing to harm her.'

Yes, he did love Verity. His voice had softened and he actually used my name as he appealed to me.

'Did Verity say she'd met me?' I'd been longing

to ask this, and I took my opportunity now that he looked less forbidding.

His face closed up again at once. 'She informed me that she had met the daughter of an old colleague of mine, and then showed me your name in her programme. I was not, therefore, surprised to receive your letter.'

'You tried to stop her going to the show, didn't you?'

'Naturally!' he snapped, but then, almost unwillingly, he added, 'Verity was very taken with your performance.'

However, before I had time to feel pleased, he recollected himself and continued: 'But, as I emphasized, Verity has no idea as to your identity, and that's how things must stay. She's just a happy, normal schoolgirl. Why do anything to make her aware of the darker side of life?'

My father scarcely had the knack of choosing his words tactfully.

'I don't exactly see myself as the darker side of life,' I said unpleasantly.

He flushed. 'No, that was not very well put. Perhaps I should just say that I don't want her childhood to end abruptly. As it would if she were to find out about you.'

Speaking about Verity, his face relaxed again, and I could understand why Maggie had fancied him. He was very handsome and still quite young, not the middle-aged man of my imagination.

'Don't you want to know anything about me?' I said, leaning forward. 'I'm your daughter too. Is protecting Verity all you can think about?'

His mouth tightened. 'Naturally, protecting my family is my first consideration.'

I reminded myself not to be hurt. 'Fair enough,'

I said. I'd had the stupid idea of telling him about my good notice. 'Anyway, if we're not going to meet again, it's scarcely worth the trouble of finding out about me, is it?'

He looked pained. 'I didn't choose to have things happen this way,' he said. 'Now that they have, I want to minimize the damage.'

Damage to whom? If I turned my head slightly, I could see Dorinda, a tiny spot of colour against the grass, and Tilda playing with her. I remembered Jimmy's words. I didn't have to let my father hurt me.

My father was finally looking at me directly, the only other person I'd ever met with navy-blue eyes.

'Please, Iris, I've no alternative but to ask you to leave Verity alone. She's a happy little girl, with a loving family. How could you consider taking that away from her? What do you have to offer instead? She's your sister, yes, but please don't hurt her because of a mistake I made years ago.'

For the first time since we'd sat down together I felt a link with my father. He was looking at me perfectly openly now, asking me for something I could scarcely refuse.

Verity was my little sister, and all I wanted was for her to be happy. I'd tried to behave like a true sister towards Janine and failed ridiculously, but now I had a second chance with my real sister. For her sake, I would give up something I wanted, something I wanted far more than a good notice – the chance to love her.

I sat up straight. I was glad I was wearing a black dress, and that I'd put my hair up. I was properly dressed for my grand gesture. I would renounce my relationship with Verity for ever.

Before I began my speech I allowed myself to

picture her for one last time. She'd looked so eager and sweet, with her red hair falling round her shoulders, and she'd been regarding me with such admiration, almost as though I were a real star instead of another schoolgirl.

I tried to imagine what it must be like to be Verity, just as I'd once tried to imagine myself as Janine's mother. What was it like, being the only child of such uptight parents, a mother who had to be protected from reality at all costs, and a self-important, self-righteous father? If I were in her position, wouldn't I *want* to have an older sister – especially a sister whom I already admired, and who was ready to love me?

When the answer hit me, it was as though I'd been thrown something light and soft and wonderfully unexpected. Of course she'd want me! If I were Verity, I'd *need* a sister, I wouldn't let our relationship be flung away just to satisfy a bunch of secretive, hypocritical adults.

From my father's puzzled and slightly alarmed expression I knew that my sudden brilliant smile had caught him off balance. It wasn't what he was expecting.

I sat forward, facing him, and put my elbows on the table. I knew exactly what to do, just as, occasionally, when I was acting, I knew exactly, with complete certainty, how to behave.

'I'll tell you what I'm going to do,' I said. I noticed that, as I spoke, I sounded as self-assured as Maggie. 'How old's Verity now?'

'She's only just thirteen.'

'I'm seventeen. In four years' time, when she's the age I am now, I'm going to get in touch with her and tell her that we're half-sisters. If she wants to have me as her sister, then I'll be there. And if she doesn't, I promise I'll never bother her again. It'll be her decision.'

My father fell back in his chair. 'You're prepared to break up a family—'

'Is your family so weak that I've got the power to break it?'

He didn't answer me at once, but kept shaking his head and swallowing. Finally he said: 'But what about my wife?'

'It's up to Verity whether she tells her or not.'

'That's an enormous responsibility to place on a young person!'

'It'll help her to grow up. She can't be your little girl for ever.'

Unlike Maggie, whom shock had rendered expressionless, my father's whole face was twitching and jerking with anger and distress. 'You're a wayward, trouble-making neurotic! You're completely undisciplined—'

'No, father,' I said, standing up. 'It's you who were undisciplined. Only once, but in your case, once was enough. I'm glad we've met. Thank you for the salad. Goodbye.'

I replaced my chair neatly beside the table. Then I turned round and walked out of the café. As I passed them I was aware of one or two of the old ladies nodding in a satisfied way at having seen such a handsome father and daughter eating together.

Once outside, I leant against the wall. I felt fantastic, yet I was shaking all over. I shut my eyes and tried to think of something calming, but all I could see was Verity's face as she disappeared into the crowd. What would happen in four years' time?

When I opened my eyes I immediately saw Tilda, waiting in the park. She must've been watching the café door for me because she was waving eagerly.

I crossed the road and joined her on Dorinda's blanket.

'Well, well, what happened? Was it OK? Or was he awful to you?' Tilda was regarding me anxiously.

'Sort of awful, sort of OK,' I said slowly. 'He probably hates me now, but it was worth it.'

I told her what I'd done.

Tilda leant back on her elbows. 'Iris, you were inspired.'

'It's odd, you know, but I was. I suddenly knew exactly what to do. It's happened to me before, like on the first night of *Anaesthesia*, but never in real life.'

Tilda touched my knee. 'You know, if Verity doesn't want you for a sister, she'll be daft as a brush.'

'What?'

'I think it's Scots for downright stupid.'

'Well, she might not want me.' I sighed. 'It's not as though my father did. He just seems to blame me for existing.'

'That's not your fault. It's not you he's rejecting, but what he did as a young man. He's scared, Iris; you're reminding him of something he'd rather forget.'

'Do you know, he actually called me "the darker side of life"?'

'Oh no! I don't believe it!' Tilda began to laugh, putting her arms round her knees and rocking backwards and forwards. 'I'm sorry, I'm sorry, I shouldn't laugh, but just where is he coming from? No-one thinks like that nowadays.'

'He was so *pompous*,' I said, half indignant, half laughing. 'All I wanted was the chance to get to know Verity.'

'And if Verity's got any sense, you will.'

'Maybe. But I've got to wait four years.' My elation was dying down. I sighed and began to play with Dorinda, tickling her fat little hands with a daisy. 'And in the end I might not be her idea of a sister.'

'Mmm,' said Tilda. 'Actually, I've got something to ask you. I was saving it in case you needed to be cheered up.' She paused as dramatically as Jimmy would've done. 'Jimmy and I were wondering if you'd be one of Dorinda's godmothers.'

'Tilda!' I felt as though a crown had been placed upon my head. 'Oh Tilda, I'd love to, of course I would, it's such an *honour* – are you sure?'

'Of course we're sure! The other godmother's my best friend from college, but Jimmy and I thought that Dorinda ought to have someone younger as well, so that when she's a teenager and totally despises us for being old and stuffy and out-of-date, she can go round to your place and moan.'

'If that's all I have to do, I think I can cope.'

'You'll be wonderful.'

Tilda leant forward and kissed me formally. Then we hugged and laughed.

'Do you know,' she said, letting me go, 'I'm almost looking forward to this christening. It's not what we'd have done if we only had to please ourselves, but Jimmy's family would be so upset if we didn't have her christened – especially his grandfather. He's Spanish, and very traditional.'

I began to laugh. 'I know it's awful, but when I first met Jimmy I thought he'd chosen the name Garcia because it's so romantic, and he was really Jimmy Postlethwaite or something.'

'Oh no,' said Tilda, groaning. 'That serves him right. That's exactly the sort of impression he makes on people.'

'But we all adore him!' I protested.

'Well, he doesn't deserve it. His grandfather's really the romantic one. He was shipwrecked on the coast of Cornwall, fell in love with a Cornish girl, and never went home.'

'Oh, that *is* romantic – what a hero!'

'Look, there's your hero coming.'

Tilda pointed over my shoulder and I turned round. Randal was coming down the hill towards us, a head taller than anyone else on the street, the rare Scottish sunlight shining on his blond hair.

'He's come to check up on you. He's afraid your father's murdered you in order to protect his guilty secret.'

We leant against one another, giggling.

'No chance,' I said. 'You can't murder someone in a café with frilly curtains.'

I wondered where Verity and I would meet in four years' time.

Randal waved.

'Oh, Tilda,' I said. 'Doesn't one ever get to be completely happy?'

'Not often,' she said, 'so make the most of what you've got.'

I waved back.

Randal. Tilda. The wonderful review. The sun shining on the little patch of tired city grass.

Dorinda, already old enough to sense that my attention had been withdrawn, gave a cry. I bent down and picked her up.

Dorinda, my god-daughter. That was a start. I might get to be a sister yet.

THE END